D0616363

THE AUCTIO
FOOL...BUT EASY TO KILL.

Frederick Hardy had spent the morning pounding his gavel to the tune of big money. Now he was settling down to a well-deserved lunch. He reached for a special bottle that stood on the sideboard. The dark green glass gave off a sinister glow as he poured the mix-ture over his salad, but he didn't notice. Greedily, he stuffed his mouth, licked his lips, and fell down dead. As screams and cries filled the room, no one noticed a hand reach out quickly from the shadows to seize the one shred of murderous evidence...

THE GIMMEL
FLASK

Scene of the Crime® Mysteries

Murder Ink® Mysteries

A Murder Ink.® Mystery

THE GIMMEL FLASK

FLASK

Douglas Clark

A DELL BOOK

Published by
Dell Publishing Co., Inc.
1 Dag Hammarskjold Plaza
New York, New York 10017

This work was first published in Great Brtiain
by Victor Gollancz Ltd.

Dell ® TM 681510, Dell Publishing Co., Inc.

ISBN: 0-440-13160-x

Printed in the United States of America
U.S.A.
First printing—April 1982

THE GIMMEL
FLASK

CHAPTER I

The first Tuesday in the month. A grey March day.
Grey and cloudy, but with a mildness about it that
made the people of Limpid aware that spring might
not be too far away. Today, no wind blew down the
market hill. No waste paper scurried across the open
triangle below the church where, on Thursdays, the
stalls were erected and Limpid woke to a commercial
bustle entirely lacking at all other times except, perhaps, on Saturday mornings.

But the first Tuesday in the month was special for
Limpid. On these days, the town's leading firm of
auctioneers and estate agents held their monthly sale
in the Corn Exchange. Hardy, Williams and Lamont—three bold-faced men, all flashy and used to
high-living on the easy pickings of their calling—dom-
inated these monthly gatherings. From 10 am to 4
pm, with no break at lunchtime, they occupied the
rostrum in turn, to knock down the lots to be auctioned.

Limpid was a buyer's delight. A market town in the
centre of a vast agricultural area, it had no rivals
among the villages and hamlets that dotted this part

of East Anglia. But the farmhouses and cottages, as well as the dwellings of Limpid itself, yielded an almost limitless store of antique furniture, pottery and bric-a-brac. Much of this—some of it turned out of the houses where it had lain for decades in order to make way for modernisation, some of it the household effects of the recently deceased—found its way to the Hardy, Williams and Lamont sales. A permanent 'ring' attended; dealers from Cambridge, Ipswich, Colchester and Norwich were always there. The London dealers had their local spies. On viewing day, always the Monday before the sale, these spies sniffed round the items as they were carried into the Corn Exchange and laid out or stacked in handling order. If there was anything that appeared likely to interest the London dealers, a phone call would either bring a buyer down in person or result in a commission for the spy—an order to enter the bidding up to a limit fixed by the dealer.

Richard Benson was a collector, not a dealer. As he slowly made his way down the market hill on the Corn Exchange side, he was thinking about his hobby. It had never become a disease with him: a sickness which drove him on to amass hundreds of articles simply for the sake of hoarding treasures. He prided himself on an intellectual approach. Had he ever been asked to express his aim or even his approach to his collection, he would have claimed that his hobby was an intelligent, probably an admirable, occupation in that he sought for beauty in the work of men's hands; that he studied history from the original sources which our forebears had left behind; that he revealed the social trends and customs on which modern civilisation has built, not, alas, always for the better; and somewhere among this list he would inevitably have murmured the word 'mores' simply because it is a word beloved by historians and art critics, and he read much of both.

"Morning, Mr Benson. Going along to the sale then, I see." Benson stopped. Theraby always stood just outside his shop door if trade was slack and the weather was warm enough to allow it. His shop was a long-fronted, shallow building, the result of combining two former shops adjacent to each other. It was an old-fashioned clothier's—men's wear at one end, women's wear at the other. The heavy mahogany counters carried screwed-in brass measures and stood in front of a whole wall of pigeon-holes, each one filled with a different item. Though a young woman could not buy a smart ball gown from Theraby, she would be able to choose the loveliest of woollen bed-jackets for her granny's birthday, or a thorn-proof skirt; while men could buy off-the-peg west of England tweed slacks that would last a lifetime. Benson often patronised Theraby. It was the only shop in Limpid that could supply him with a stiff collar and Theraby the only outfitter he knew who didn't sneer at the thought of a man still wearing braces instead of tying himself up tight in the middle like a wasp in corsets.

"Morning Theraby. Have you heard what the Committee decided last night?"

"I've heard. The answer is nothing—so far."

"So you don't know whether your premises will survive or not?"

"They discussed it and then referred it back to the full Council, whatever that means."

"At least it means that your objection has caused

them to think again. Councillors in a town this size have to think twice if petition carries over three thousand names. Dammit, there's only seven thousand souls in the whole place."

"I know, Mr. Benson. And I want to thank you for organising that for me. I'm sure it helped a lot."

"Think nothing of it, Theraby. There are well over a hundred buildings of architectural merit in this town. Obvious places like the Moot Hall, the Abbey Cottages and so on have preservation orders on them because they're beamed. Studwork is preserved, but places like the Corn Exchange, which are fine examples of Victorian architecture with a lot of outstanding ironwork, are ignored. And that's not right. Your shop is old, but none the worse for that. In addition it's an amenity. You give good service and always have done. If they demolish your shop, they demolish your service, and God knows there's little enough of that about these days."

Theraby pushed his mole-grey felt hat back a bit on his bald head. His was a nondescript face. There was just too much flesh on the cheeks and the pores were deep and coarse. The nose was bulbous and had a few hairs growing on the rounded end. His eyebrows were grey and thick and great sheaves of hair grew out of his ears, but in spite of his age there was nothing rheumy about his eyes, which were wide and bright. He was, thought Benson, a man incapable of expression with any feature except his eyes. Now they had assumed a glint of interest and intelligence where previously they had been quiescent. "You've a good point there, Mr Benson. I'll use it if I may. Destroy these premises and you destroy the service. I'll have a placard made and put in the shop."

"Tell me, Theraby, have you discovered who is behind this campaign to demolish your home and shop?"

Theraby always wore grey. His coat overall was grey denim, his trousers charcoal-grey worsted. His tie was grey. The whole man was nothing more than a part of the dark interior of his shop brought out into the daylight for inspection, much as his customers, when choosing goods, brought them to the shop doorway in order to see the exact shade and texture.

"I'd not heard anybody was behind it, Mr Benson—except the Council. They want to make a compulsory purchase so that they can build some flash supermarket which they'll lease for a big rent. That's what's behind it."

"Where did you learn that from?"

"Fred Hardy, and he's a councillor, so he should know."

"Hardy, Williams and Lamont's offices are only three or four doors up from you. They're in an old house of no architectural merit whatsoever. Have they received a compulsory purchase order?"

"Not yet. But Fred Hardy says they're expecting one any time."

"I see. Well, Theraby, don't give up hope too soon. I must push on. It's ten to ten by the church clock. I want a place in the crowd where I can see and be seen."

"Buying, are you?"

"Maybe. Depends on prices. If things go up much more I'll be selling instead of buying."

Benson raised his stick in farewell. He was a man of middle age and middle height. He wore a nail-bag hat, a pepper and salt jacket as bright and clean as a new pin. His grey-green worsted trousers were impeccably creased and his brown shoes gleamed. The patina shaded light on the raised portions of the leather at toe-caps and heels, but darkened off almost to black elsewhere. He wore unlined gloves, a striped shirt and a navy blue tie. He limped as he went, swinging one leg wide and stiff.

Must give these shoes a wash in milk, he thought, as he went past the gown shop below Theraby's. Toilet soap and milk—the old saddler's trick to remove unwanted polish where it had built up into black areas. Toilet soap because mildness was needed. Milk because it didn't ruin the shine, leaving, rather, a thin varnish of its own on which to rebuild.

He stood aside to let pass two women coming down the four steps that led from the East Anglian Bank. He raised his hat courteously. Mrs Horbium was known to him. She dabbled in objets d'art, her aim seeming to be a desire to amass hundreds of examples of whatever she could lay her hands on in the way of glassware and pottery, irrespective of period or original purpose. The other woman he did not know, but yet her face seemed familiar. She was younger, much younger, than her companion and decidedly more interesting to a man accustomed to the study of beauty in works of art.

"Good morning, Mr Benson. You'll be at the sale, I suppose?"

It was an unnecessary question. Mrs Horbium knew the answer. So she did not pause to receive it, but swept on, turning left towards the entrance to the Corn Exchange. Benson followed slowly. Mrs Horbium was a large woman. A bouncy large woman. This morning she was all in black. As she went she rolled slightly; a sway induced by the impetus of her weight, which never seemed quite to recover from one sideways movement before a step forward required it to go the other way. Beside her, her companion seemed slight and slim, though Benson, who was a great admirer of women's legs, noted that the calves were firm and beautifully shaped and the feet well and neatly shod in as attractive a pair of shoes as he'd seen on a woman in years.

Next, the green shop front of the dairy, where they sold not only dairy produce but cream cakes, among which the meringues were notable not only for taste and filling but for size, too. He stopped by the door and called to the woman behind one of the counters: "Keep me two meringues for four o'clock, Bessie, please."

"Going to give Mrs Taylor a treat, are you?"

"And myself."

Mrs Taylor was his housekeeper. At least he called her that and she accepted it, but she was, in fact, a daily woman who came on Mondays to launder, Tuesdays to clean, Thursdays to do the marketing and Fridays to tidy up for the weekend and—as she put it—'do him a good big bake to see him through'. The good big bake was of plain food. Lots of scones, a sponge cake, beef pie, apple pie and sausage rolls. The list varied little. Benson was a man of habit and Mrs Taylor's culinary repertoire was limited in variety though unsurpassed in quality.

A dry-cleaner's next. One of those half-shops with a door at an angle to another half-shop, inset in the original doorway. Benson didn't like the firm. It was one of a chain that put disclaimers in small print on all their documents so that no matter what happened to a garment while in their hands, the blame was not theirs. Loss or damage or just plain bad workmanship were all the same. Benson preferred the shop on the High Street that the proprietors of the Limpid Steam Laundry had run for over sixty years. There, if anything went wrong, one called Harry Box, the working owner, and told him about it. Then something was done—though, now he came to think about it, very little did go wrong in Harry Box's works because Harry was there himself to see it didn't.

The other half of the divided shop was owned by a comparative newcomer. A young man called Jack Racine, a photographer who sold cameras and took good pictures of weddings and social gatherings, as well as amazingly good portraits. Benson liked Racine, who was a blond giant with a pretty young wife who— so rumour had it—had at one time been a photographer's model. Benson suspected the rumour meant by that that Jill Racine had posed nude. If so, he reckoned she would have been a jolly good eyeful. Racine had, not long before, photographed Benson's collection, piece by piece, because the insurance company and the police had suggested it to make description and identification easier in case of theft. Jill had come with her husband and had endeared herself to Benson not simply by her looks, but by her obvious rapture over his treasures. She had fetched and carried for her husband throughout the session, but all the time she had handled the items with loving care. Benson had scented a nascent interest in his hobby and on several occasions since their first meeting had chatted to her about antiques. Jack Racine was good tempered. He had arrived in Limpid prepared to work hard to make a success of his little business. Benson liked that.

He had recommended Racine to several of his acquaintances, many of whom, he reflected, could never be dealt with successfully by anyone but a good tempered man.

Benson tapped on the window as he passed. Jill, who was dusting a pair of binoculars, looked up and waved. She mouthed some message, then held up both hands with fingers widespread. She followed this by a Churchillian two fingered gesture. And inclined her head sideways in the direction of the Corn Exchange. Benson took it to mean that she would look in at the saleroom at twelve o'clock, presumably when Jack returned from some job. He nodded his understanding of the message, lifted his stick in farewell and took the last dozen steps to the door of the Exchange. As he arrived, the clock in the church tower struck ten o'clock.

Two or three large vehicles stood at the curb. One belonged to a firm of local furnishers who prided themselves on being both modern and antique as regards stock. Obviously they had their eye on quite a few pieces. They liked gate-leg tables and sets of dining chairs with carvers. Benson knew from his preview that there were several such lots. The vehicle behind this was nameless, but he recognised the blue tilt. It belonged to the auctioneers' porters. They gathered up the sale items in it. Now three men in their shirt sleeves, with green baize aprons, were offloading some last minute additions to the list—bulky stuff, a double bed and a couple of old heavy wardrobes, a marble-topped washstand and matching dressing table in bird's-eye maple.

The third van he did not recognise. It had the air of an interloper and the number plates to prove it was not on home ground. Some dealer was after something. There was rather a fine chiffonier in there and a couple of horse trough wine coolers. . . .

He limped up the steps.

Benson was fond of the Corn Exchange. It was still used for its original purpose on Thursdays, and farmers from round about did actually offer samples of grain within its walls and transact various other deals to do with their businesses. But a few other sidelines had crept in. Notably the sale of pullets, eggs and butter. There was the cattle market for livestock, and Hardy, Williams and Lamont conducted sales there every Thursday. But the Corn Exchange was still a centre in its own right, and when not in use for its original purpose and auctions such as the one being held today, it offered a venue for the Chrysanthemum Society Annual Show, The Cage Bird Society Show, and all manner of other exhibitions and demonstrations.

The only permanent occupants of the Corn Exchange were a pair of house martins. As soon as he was up the steps and through the outer door, Benson looked for them. They perched high on the great crossbeams of the lofty hall whenever people flocked in. But if they weren't to be seen there—motionless little black and white dots close together—Benson knew he might spot them at their window. All the windows in the exchange were high. That is, their sills were a good ten feet above the floor. The narrow, leaded panes ran up very high, particularly those opposite the door, because the pitch of the roof allowed them—particularly the centre one of the three—to rise close up under the apex. This was the house-martins' window. At the top, a semicircular

storm vent was always left partly open for them, and
here it was they fluttered in and out. Benson saw
them there this morning hovering, apparently in
slight dismay at the noise made by the crowd: an in-
trusion they had experienced many times before, but
to which it took them an hour or so to reaccustom
themselves.

He could barely squeeze through the inner door.
Here a crowd of people always congregated: the ones
who were only intending to stay a short time and had
no wish to get further into the hall, deep in the
crowd from which it was often difficult to extricate
oneself. He managed to round the knot of chattering
citizens and found himself in calmer waters. He
paused a moment to look about him. The towering
roof fascinated him, with its great iron crossbeams
and screw-ties decorated with casts of wheat sheaves.
These latter had been picked out in gold which stood
out vividly against the green paintwork. The walls
were cream-washed down to the dado, and below
that, green paint again.

The auctioneer's dais with its chair and table was
in the centre of the vast room, facing a side wall. Behind the dais was stacked the furniture; a great higgledy-piggledy heap of it running the length of the
hall and coming out almost to the halfway point. In
front of the dais was a row of trestle tables; a great
looping row which ran in a curve from the end of the
furniture heap nearest the door, to a point at the far
end below the martins' exit. On these tables were the
small articles—silver, pottery and glassware. In front
of the tables were the only seats for those attending.
The custom was to range the couches and sofas to be

offered for sale along the lengths of the tables to seat
the elderly, almost as if they were in the front row of
the stalls. Behind the sofas was the promenade: standing room only for the majority, except that on the
long wall facing the dais were ranged the desks of the
corn chandlers. These were the narrow, sloping-
topped, working desks at which one stood to write.
They formed a long base on which rolls of bedding,
mattresses and curtains were piled, ready for sale.
Young people attending the auction climbed atop
these and got not only a good view of the proceedings, but a soft seat, too.

This lay-out gave the auctioneer's men a long narrow area of movement for displaying the wares; and
at the end opposite the door it left room for their
clerk to set up a table and conduct his business of log-
ging the sales and taking the cash. Benson knew this
lay-out of old. He knew exactly where the ring would
congregate, a dozen or so strong, straight opposite the
auctioneer and occupying a disproportionate space
for their numbers. As he passed behind them, he
noted they were busy with their catalogues, marking
in what each was intent on buying. It was a cartel.
Dealer A would refrain from bidding against dealer B
for lot number five if dealer B would reciprocate over
lot twelve. And so on. Between them they sought to
carve up the sale, covering every worthwhile article
with a buying plan calculated to rob the vendors, to
cut out lay buyers, and to line their own pockets with
profits of, sometimes, many hundred per cent. Benson
also knew, however, that the machinations of the ring
were no match for the lay buyer among smaller items.
A woman really determined to buy some article she

had set her heart on was always willing to go a little higher than the members of the ring. They had an eye to profit. They had to buy below what they knew they could sell for in their shops. She only had one objective—ownership. She usually achieved it for less than she would pay in the open market.

Benson passed behind the ring and chose an open square yard of floor. He glanced at his watch. Five past ten. Everything running true to form. The auctioneers were not the people to start promptly and run the risk of low bids before all those intending to come had arrived. There was always ten minutes' grace for latecomers. He looked around. Mrs Horbium had managed to get a seat on a sofa. With a mental smile, he noted that it was the best and cleanest sofa in the row—a cream and crimson brocaded settee occupied by three elderly women who were now crushed unmercifully together by Mrs Horbium's vast bottom. She still wore her large brimmed black hat, while from behind, the long, pendant jet earrings seemed to be in perpetual motion as their many facets caught the light one after another and gleamed momentarily. For a moment he could not see Mrs Horbium's companion; then he spotted her, edging her way back from the clerk's desk to stand behind the sofa. She had a pristine catalogue in her hand, so he guessed the purpose of her visit.

Fred Hardy took the dais first. He was a heavily built man with short legs and twiddle toes. He wore a mid-grey suit and a fawn-green trilby which he didn't attempt to remove. It was pulled well down over his brow, reminding Benson that somebody had once said that if all our sins were writ large on our foreheads, some would feel the need to wear their hats down to eye level.

"Ladies and gentlemen, if we don't get on we shan't get through today." Hardy sounded petulant: as if he were accusing those before him of causing the delay, and not his own carefully planned cupidity.

"Lot one."

There would be a few rubbishy lots first, just to give the big spenders and latecomers even more of an opportunity to get there.

"Three pails, a handbroom and various small brushes. Who'll start me at one pound?"

Silence.

"Come along, ladies and gentlemen. One pound?"

"Ninety pence? Eighty? Seventy? Seventy I am bid. Any advance on seventy pence for the pails and brushes? Seventy pence then, it is." Hardy looked up. "Mrs . . . ?"

"Faber," said a voice.

"Mrs Faber." The name and amount were written in the first space of the perforated book. Ten spaces to a page. When full, the page would be torn out, and handed to one of the porters who would carry it across to the clerk. The clerk, in turn, would make out separate invoices for each lot. The money would start to come in shortly after the first page was full.

"Lot two."

"Lot three."

"Lot four."

They were knocked down quickly. Rolls of lino, slip mats, an old knifebox full of bits and pieces.

A caudle cup was put up. Benson guessed Hardy didn't know what he was selling. The ring did. One of them went to four pounds for it and smirked his pleasure at the bargain. All members of the ring marked their catalogues with the price. There'd be a bit of financial settling to do at the end of the day.

Benson glanced at his watch. Hardy was up to schedule. He reckoned to average about two minutes a lot. Ten past eleven and lot thirty-five was being displayed by the head porter, who was carrying it along the line of sofas. A chocolate pot, a caster and a teapot of English seventeenth-century silver. This time Hardy knew he was selling something of value— probably because it was silver, not because of its age and beauty. He waited until the porter's slow procession ended.

"You need me to tell you, ladies and gentlemen, that we have a fine lot here. It came from the home of the late Mrs Acton-Stuart. Solid silver. Who'll start me at a hundred pounds?"

Silence. The ring lay low. The housewives looked at each other, grimaced and shook their heads as much as to say that such a starting price put paid to their hopes of a bargain round about the five pound mark.

Benson was interested. He didn't want the lot, but he knew it. Had inspected and admired it at the Acton-Stuart home. It was worth the hundred and a lot more besides. He didn't want the estate to suffer. Jeremy Acton-Stuart, the grandson and heir, was in Northern Ireland with his regiment. Benson felt the least he could do was to prevent the boy being too badly fleeced by the ring. He raised his catalogue slightly.

"One hundred I am bid on my right. One hundred

for the silver." Pause. "Come along, gentlemen, save my time and yours."

Benson, who was watching the ring closely, just caught the flicker of movement.

"One hundred and five."

Benson reckoned he could safely afford to push them to at least a hundred and fifty. He re-entered.

"One hundred and ten on my right."

Glances from the members of the ring to see who was against them. Benson made no attempt to hide his interest. They knew him. They also knew that if he was prepared to bid, their own estimates of the value of the lot were not at fault.

"One hundred and fifteen."

"Twenty . . . twenty-five. . . ."

Benson made his last bid at one-fifty. The ring chalked up a winner at a hundred and fifty-five.

Benson was hoping lot 52 would be reached before midday. He was hoping for a bargain here; not for his own collection, but he had thought as soon as he saw them that the set of little pewter Baluster measures would be a nice gift for Jill Racine, to start her off on her expressed intention of collecting once she could afford to do so. The measures would go well in her rather bare sitting room and would need no cleaning. They were flat-lidded, in a graded set from half a gill up to the quart. Benson was delighted by the fact that this set boasted Scots shell thumb pieces, which are normally associated with the Glasgow and Edinburgh dome-lidded, pear-shaped measures. He wondered if anybody else here would have appreciated this rather unique feature. Somehow, he doubted it. Measures are more of interest to collectors than to dealers who, if they do dabble, prefer to go for the lidded, pot-bellied types or the harvester measures with their more flowing curves and haystack shapes.

Hardy obviously felt he had lost time over the silver. He pushed ahead quickly. Benson knew Hardy would want to reach at least lot 60 by twelve o'clock when, his two hour stint finished, he would hand over to either Williams or Lamont and make his way to the Swan and Cygnets for a couple of hefty gins and a big lunch. But today it was going to be a near thing. Lot 52 came up at eight minutes to twelve.

"Set of measures," said Hardy. "Beer and spirits. Now all you publicans, just the thing for you. Any landlords in the house? No? Who'll give me ten pounds? A complete set in pewter, gentlemen. Useful, these measures."

Pause.

"Eight?"

Pause.

"Do you want me to give them away?"

Voice in the crowd: "Yes."

"Very well. Six."

"I'll start at four," said Mrs Horbium in a loud, harsh voice.

Benson cursed gently to himself. With Mrs Horbium against him, the bidding would go too high for a gift for Jill. The last thing he wanted to do was to embarrass the girl with an expensive present. Besides, like the ring, if Mrs Horbium knew he was against her she would know the measures were worth something and would press ahead all the harder. Ah, well! There might be some fun to be had. He raised his catalogue.

"Five," said Hardy.

"No," said Benson. "Four twenty-five."

Hardy glared, but could not refute it. The bids went up by tenpence a time below two pounds, by 25p between two pounds and five pounds, by 50p up to ten pounds and thereafter by one pound to fifty pounds, two pounds to a hundred, and five pounds above a hundred. Benson was a stickler for the sale rules.

"Four twenty-five, Benson," snapped Hardy.

It had the desired effect. Mrs Horbium came again, so did Benson. Then the dealers woke up to the fact that if the two local collectors were slogging it out, they themselves might be missing something. One of them entered the bidding. Benson immediately dropped out and let Mrs Horbium buy at thirteen pounds.

Benson contented himself with buying, a few minutes later, an enamel wine label. It was not a Battersea specimen, but a slightly coarser product made, he guessed, at either Wednesbury or Bilston, although the design, he imagined, was taken from one by Francois Ravenet. At any rate the colours were pleasant but, to his surprise, they had not caught the eye of the jackdaw-ish Mrs Horbium. He'd had a clear field. He could honestly tell Jill he'd got it for nothing and she would be the more pleased because of it.

When the auctioneer's sheet went across to the clerk, Benson edged his way to the desk.

"Hello, Mr Benson. You got lot fifty-five. Do you want it now?"

"Please."

The clerk despatched a porter to fetch the wine label, while Benson paid. "You're not leaving us now, are you, Mr Benson?"

"No. I bought the enamel for a friend. I'm going to deliver it now."

"See you later then, perhaps."

"Perhaps."

As he left the desk, Benson wrapped the little label very carefully in the clean handkerchief he had in his pocket. A moment or two after he arrived at his former position, Jill's voice said, "Hello," very conspiratorially in his ear. Almost at the same time, Hardy announced that Williams would take over the business of selling.

"Where have they got to?" asked Jill.

"Lot sixty-three is next."

"Good."

"Are you intending to bid?"

"Or to get you to bid for me."

"Not a hope," replied Benson. "You learn to do it for yourself, young lady. Besides, I'm too well-known. If I start bidding some people here might think the item to be valuable if it attracts me."

"Oh, it isn't in the least valuable. Not like that."

"What is it?"

"Lot sixty-nine."

"A standard lamp with shade?"

"Yes. I'd like it for the sitting room."

"Right. Have you made up you mind what is the highest amount you're prepared to spend?"

"I thought three pounds."

"Splendid. Now whatever happens, don't be tempted to go above that figure. And don't start bidding at the figure he asks first."

"But I might miss it."

"Impossible. They wait for ages to make sure somebody isn't going to raise the last bid."

"Lot sixty-three," droned Williams, and then cleared his throat. "A modern sideboard in teak. Worth every penny of seventy pounds in the shops. I'll start at thirty."

"Watch," whispered Benson.

"Twenty-five, then."

The sideboard eventually went for fifteen pounds to the local furniture shop. "Secondhand now added to modern and antique," murmured Benson. "Did you learn the lesson?"

"Yes."

"Good girl."

"Lot sixty-nine," said Williams. "Standard lamp in oak with round base and turned stem. The pink shade goes with it and it's even got a bulb, hasn't it Bert?"

"Dunno whether it works or not," said Bert lugubriously as he held the lamp aloft. "I 'aven't tried it."

A laugh from the crowd greeted this remark and Williams said: "In that case I'm not selling the lamp as in working order. Where shall we start, ladies and gentlemen? Lamp and shade. Who'll say two pounds?"

Benson kept a light pressure on Jill's arm to prevent eagerness running away with her. No takers.

"One pound then. Let's save the time, please."

"One pound I'm bid."

"Now," whispered Benson, and Jill put up her hand.

"One ten . . . twenty . . . thirty . . . forty. . . ."

"Steady," whispered Benson, "you're letting it run away with you. Who has it?"

"She has. Not me."

"Give it a moment. Let her see you're not sure it's worth it. It will breed doubt in her mind. Now, bid."

"One fifty," said Williams, impatient to get along. "Any more? One fifty it is." He looked across. "Mrs Racine?" Jill nodded eagerly.

"Congratulations," said Benson. "Now remember, start a fast run like that and you're going down a slope on which you're unable to stop."

"Thank you."

"Are you after anything else?"

"No, I've got to get back to get the lunch. Jack's minding the shop."

"Come along and collect your buy. It's light enough to carry the few paces home."

As he saw her safely on to the pavement, past the increased lunchtime crowd at the door, Benson handed her the little handkerchief-wrapped parcel. "Here's a little present for you. Nobody else put in a bid, so I was able to get it for a nominal amount. Let me have the nuffer back some time."

"You *are* nice." She stood on tiptoe and kissed his cheek. "I'm not going to look at it till I have a few spare moments, then I'll really be able to enjoy the mystery."

He raised his hat and she was gone, shouldering her way through the skewed door of the little shop. Benson returned to the Corn Exchange.

The one item he was really interested in was 131. If all went well, it should come up soon after the third auctioneer, Lamont, took the dais. But Benson was

taking no chances. He had known these auctioneers—
unethically—bring an item forward at the request of
some interested dealer who had wanted to get away
early. He had to guard against that.

When he again reached his position he noted that
the ring had halved in size. This was usual. Half of
them went off to lunch at a time, leaving the others
to mind the shop. Mrs Horbium, however, had gone.
This was not unexpected by Benson. Mrs Horbium
was not one to forgo her lunch no matter what. He
guessed, too, that she liked a snooze after it. If she
were not to come back, so much the better. One probable competitor out of the reckoning. Her companion
had gone, too. Benson wished he could recall whom
she reminded him of. He was surprised at his own interest, and wondered why what had been little more
than a fleeting glance of her should have aroused his
curiosity.

The sale dragged on. Always at this time of the day
it seemed to lose some of its impetus. The initial excitement was over and the proceedings had settled
into a routine. Quite an efficient routine, really. Benson admitted that at least he must pay the three auctioneer partners their due for the smooth running of
their sales. He could think of very little else about
them for which he could find a word of praise.

At two o'clock and lot 127, Williams gave way to
Lamont. Lamont was by far the youngest of the partners. He had been articled to the firm earlier and had
stayed on to become the junior partner. Now he was
beginning to show that he felt the effects of comparatively easy money. He had married a girl who, Benson suspected, had had nothing in early life and now

demanded everything in compensation for her years
of deprivation. Their house was big. Lamont had not
overtly 'fiddled' this, but he had managed to buy it,
not through the normal channels, but at an execu-
tor's sale where prices are notably lower than those
proposed by estate agents. Had Lamont had the selling of the house instead of the buying of it, the two
prices would have differed by many thousands of
pounds, and in this particular case, Benson was sure
'inside knowledge' had played its part. Lamont had
big ideas, also. His wife used a very large Mercedes
for fetching the bread, and the cruiser on the river
had not been bought for peanuts.

Benson had a shrewd idea that Lamont was feeling
the pinch. The man had little knowledge of antiques,
but over the last few months had tried to give the impression that he was interested. That the interest was
spurious, Benson had no doubt. Lamont had approached him several times on the subject of late, but
it was painfully apparent to the connoisseur that Lamont was more interested in prices than values. Benson wondered whether he himself was the cynic or
whether it was Lamont, when judged by Lord Dar-
lington's yardstick. Certainly Benson was cynical of
Lamont's probity, even if it were the auctioneer who
lived up to the stated definition as a man who knows
the price of everything and the value of nothing.

Lamont got under way. He used the end of his pencil for knocking. It gave a strangely thin sound after
the gavel the others had used previously. The lots between 127 and 130 were ordinary. They were sold
with no flurry. Mrs Horbium had not returned. The
first half of the ring had returned, the others were

about to go. They stood in a huddle, heads to the middle, catalogues out, pencilling in prices and buys and prospective bids. They didn't seem in the least interested in Lot 131. Benson wondered why. It was unlike them, but it could mean he would have a comparatively clear field.

"Lot 131, ladies and gentlemen. No need to describe it. It is on the table in front of me." Lamont seemed to be in a hurry. So much so that he omitted to mention a figure as a suggested starting point. "What am I bid?"

Silence.

"Four pounds." The pencil was raised to knock it down. Benson had heard no bid, seen no movement. Suspicious of what was happening, he raised his catalogue higher than usual to make certain he could not be overlooked.

Lamont saw him and nodded.

"Four twenty-five . . . four fifty."

The twenty-five bid was Benson's. Where had the four fifty come from? Again Lamont's pencil was raised. None of the usual encouraging chat from the dais. Benson again held his catalogue aloft.

"Four seventy-five . . . five pounds."

Benson had kept his eye on Lamont: had seen the almost imperceptible nod and quick glance that passed between Lamont and Bert, the head porter.

Benson again.

"Five fifty . . . six pounds."

Bert was standing quite still, his hand on top of a tallboy. He was neglecting his duties to enter the bidding. But who was he acting for?

"Six fifty . . . seven pounds."

That opening bid of four pounds—if it had been made—was suspiciously, ridiculously low. It appeared as if the figure had been agreed earlier between Bert and Lamont. But would Lamont have agreed to so low a figure just to please Bert? Benson thought not. The figure had been agreed to please Lamont.

"Seven fifty . . . eight pounds."

So, Benson figured, Bert was bidding on behalf of Lamont. Lamont out to make a killing! Lamont who had squared the ring? "Lay off lot 131 and I'll see you're all right on lots X, Y and Z." Benson thought it possible.

"Eight fifty . . . nine pounds."

Bert was still nonchalant, but Lamont was getting edgy. He was becoming too ready to slam that pencil down.

"Nine fifty . . . ten pounds."

"Eleven pounds . . . twelve pounds."

On it went. At twenty pounds Bert turned in disgust and walked towards the chest of drawers next on the list. Benson got lot 131 for twenty-one pounds. Well satisfied, he waited to hear Lamont repeat: "Benson. Twenty-one pounds." Then he edged his way towards the clerk's table. When asked by the clerk to bring over lot 131, Bert did so with bad grace. The clerk seemed oblivious of anything out of the ordinary. Benson paid and collected his property. It was rather large and heavy. He needed both hands. To free them, he hung his stick, by the handle, in his breast pocket. Slowly he wormed his way through the screen to the door. As far as he was concerned, the sale was over. It wasn't yet three o'clock and he'd be a bit early for his meringues, but Bessie wouldn't mind making them up for him while he waited.

He looked forward to the ham sandwich he'd promised himself when he got home. After all, he had missed lunch in his determination to secure lot 131.

CHAPTER II

It was exactly nine weeks later, on the first Tuesday in May, that Detective Inspector Green walked into the office of Superintendent George Masters at the Yard and uttered the one word: "Thanks."

"What for?" Masters pretended he was unaware of any reason why Green should thank him. It was difficult—or had been until the previous summer—for Green to be civil to Masters for any reason. Masters had felt an equal antipathy towards Green, but the trauma of breaking up the team that had been so successful for a number of years had caused them each to regard the other in a somewhat different light. Masters had offered to keep Green on out of sympathy. Green had agreed to stay because finding a suitable posting in his last years of service had been not only difficult but belittling. Hence Masters' sympathy. But the bond had held. Both had realised that where, formerly, they had worked one with another on sufferance, now they had chosen to stay together, and that made a difference. They had nobody to blame but themselves if it didn't work; and neither liked being blamed for anything.

From the new beginning Green had tried, and tried hard, to cooperate. Masters, watching the painful process of a leopard trying to change its spots, had in turn made the effort to treat Green as he would treat any other man. The gap had narrowed. At least Green now addressed his chief as George and in return was addressed as Greeny. But not on this particular Tuesday morning apparently. A sign, perhaps, that they were both a little embarrassed by this particular meeting. As though they had known in advance that it would take place even though both wished it wouldn't.

"What for?" Green sounded scornful—a scorn accusing Masters of pretence. "The recommendation."

"Oh, that!"

"Yes. Oh, that!"

"Has it come through?"

"Yes."

"Congratulations. Now, Detective *Chief* Inspector, if you don't mind we'll say no more about your promotion, but I am willing to take a drink off you on account of it any time you care to suggest."

"Lunchtime. Round the corner. About half twelve."

"I'll be there."

"And the other thing."

"What other thing?"

"Your fiancée."

"Wanda? What about her?"

"Don't tell me you didn't know she was inviting me and the missus down to Pilgrim's Cottage for next weekend."

"We decided we ought to be chaperoned whenever I stay there. It's the turn of you and Mrs Green to play nursemaid—if you'll accept. I'll give you a lift down on Friday, after tea."

"We're accepting, and we'll take you up on the offer of a lift."

At that moment the internal phone rang. Masters said: "Don't go. I want a word with you about sergeants." He then picked up the phone. "Masters."

"George, there's an out-of-town job for your lot. Come and see me, now please."

Masters put the phone down. "It looks as if we'll be lucky if we get our weekend off, Greeny. That was the A.C. Crime. There's an out-of-town job on."

"For us?"

Masters nodded. "Make yourself comfy for a bit. If you stay it'll save me having to find you. Rope in Sergeant Reed, too. He might as well be here from the outset."

Detective Sergeant Reed was Hill's replacement as Masters' assistant. As yet, Brant, who had been Green's assistant, had not been replaced, though he had been gone the better part of a year. This had originally been due to the uncertainty about Green's future, but at the moment it was mainly because of a shortage of manpower. It was this situation that Masters had wanted to discuss with Green. Now Green had been promoted he would get a permanent sergeant again. It would mean taking one from an inspector. The question was, whom to choose. Though Masters was willing to give Green a free hand, he was interested in the choice because, to some degree, the harmony of the team depended on it.

Reed had now settled into his new job. He had been on one or two major investigations and both

Masters and Green were satisfied with the way he was shaping.

He arrived in Masters' office looking slightly blown. A man of medium height, and wiry rather than heavily built, he was not someone on whom the eye might light instinctively. Not that he was unprepossessing. He simply had a personality that did not immediately claim notice. That he had earned promotion and then had attracted the attention and interest of a man like Masters said quite a lot for his ability at his job. But now he was puffing slightly from hurrying.

"Luggage all in, including the murder bag."

"Good lad. But why the heavy breathing?"

"After you gave me the warning order I didn't want to waste time in case the Chief got back quick and I missed something."

"Highly commendable, lad. Draw up a chair and sit down."

As Reed complied, Green offered him a cigarette from a rather crushed packet of Kensitas.

"Tell me, boy," said Green, accepting a light, "what do you know about Detective Constable Berger?"

"Berger, sir? He's a bit of a mate of mine, so I'm probably a bit prejudiced, but I reckon he's good."

"Bright?"

"Don't know about bright, so much as thorough. He's a driver A1, of course, and he's specialising in photography."

"Not dabs?"

"Not yet at any rate. But he will, once he knows all about photography. He's the sort that learns everything there is to know about one thing and then moves on to another. He reckons that if he gets a string of proficiency ratings the pressure of those alone will help him get promotion. Of course, he's passed the constable-to-sergeant tests."

"What grade?"

"Top. You knew that. I heard you asking yesterday."

"Yes, well, never mind. And keep this under your hat."

"If you say so."

The door opened and Masters came in.

"Where to this time?" asked Green.

"The market town of Limpid."

"Nice name." At one time Green would have asked: "Where the hell's that?"

"A nice town. In East Anglia. It will take us two to two and a half hours to get there. I'd prefer to brief you as we go, because I've got something to look up before we set out."

"Fair do's. Before you start, you said you wanted to talk with me."

"About sergeants? Yes, I do. Reed, make sure we've got the right maps with us and then phone both my home and Pilgrim's Cottage. Tell both my mother and Mrs Mace that I'll be out of town for a few days, but will get in touch as soon as possible. Do it from the sergeants' room, will you, please?"

After Reed had gone, Masters went across to his bookcase and took out his navy-blue bound text-book of pharmacognosy. Green, who recognised the book, said: "One of that sort, is it?"

Masters nodded, consulting the index, and then asked: "What about a sergeant for you? Any ideas? Not for this particular caper, necessarily, but for when we get back. You'll be having more administrative work to do, remember, so you don't want to hang fire."

Green sucked a tooth noisily, a habit which Masters loathed and deplored but strove to ignore for the sake of peaceful relationships. "I was going to ask your advice."

"About any particular sergeant?"

"Not a sergeant. A D.C. Chap called Berger."

Masters turned a few pages before replying. Then: "Have you discovered his standing with the promotion board?"

"He's in the bracket, okay. But I thought that until he's shoved up, he could chore for me as a D.C."

"Plain clothes, so I don't see why not. It'll save taking somebody else's sergeant from them."

"Do you know him, George?"

"Yes, I know him."

"From which reply I gather you don't think much to him."

"I'll put it this way. I'm not going to sing his praises. You can make your own mind up. But at the same time I'm willing to go so far as to say I have no objections nor reservations about Berger. On the rare occasions he has worked with me he has done his stuff thoroughly. What you will get, if you take him on, is a man who is a sticker and has a willingness to work."

"That's not bad, is it?"

"No. As long as you don't prefer a whizz-kid."

"Heaven save me from that sort."

"Fine. Go ahead and make the arrangements. See to it now if you like. I'll be a quarter of an hour reading this. You could get the written application in so that the wheels can turn while you're away."

"Done. And. . . ."

"And what?"

"Thanks . . . again."

"They wouldn't transfer him immediately," said Green, "but as he was spare, they suggested we should take him along to see if he suits us."

"You mean you want him to come to Limpid?"

"If that's okay by you."

Masters walked across to the car, Green at his side. "We've got four seats and, as I said, it's your pigeon. I don't want to influence your choice, merely to approve it from the team's point of view."

"We'll take him," decided Green.

Reed drove, working east to the A11 and A12. Berger sat beside him, quiet, as if afraid to speak. Green was in his usual nearside back seat. Masters alongside him.

Green pulled out his battered Kensitas packet. "You don't smoke, son, do you?" he asked Berger. The constable shook his head. "Good. And the Sergeant mustn't, not while driving in heavy traffic. That's a good, cheap round."

Masters had his big-bowled cadger's pipe in his hand, but made no attempt to fill it. Green, glancing at him, said: "Something's biting you. Is it this case?"

"Yes. I'll tell you about it in a few minutes, when Reed can give us a little attention."

The day was pleasantly warm and the mid-morning traffic was beginning to thin to less than rush hour proportions. Reed made good time, and Masters was pleased to note it. The area they were passing through was not the best in London, and even the eastbound road, when it eventually reached the countryside, was an unsightly mass of ribbon development in the making. It was not until they turned towards Brentwood at Gallows Corner, where they left the Southend traffic to continue its way across the flyover, that Masters felt it time to begin his briefing.

"The man who has died," he began, "is called Frederick Hardy. He was a man of fifty-eight, a town councillor of Limpid and the senior partner in the biggest firm of auctioneers and estate agents in the area."

"He'll have been well britched then," commented Green. "Estate agents—aren't they what your pal Heath calls the unacceptable face of capitalism?"

Masters felt a faint surge of anger. He had long considered Green as one of those socialists who let their credo permeate their whole lives, jaundice every action, and taint every word. The sort that paint the world grey because they must insist on bringing envy into everything. This attitude had played a large part in their earlier antipathy. So it was with some asperity and not a little untruth that Masters replied: "Heath could hardly be called a pal of mine, since I consider him to be so far left as to be one of the best socialists ever to come to power in this country. Furthermore, his comment about the unacceptable face of capitalism referred to those who made use of so-called tax havens. I should have thought that a man of your prodigious memory would have recalled the facts more exactly, and also have remembered that over the past few years quite a few of our colleagues have been engaged in unveiling some of the more unacceptable faces of socialism, particularly in the north-east. So now, can we forget politics, as we are on a non-political investigation, and turn our minds to the more mundane business of murder?"

"Crikey," said Green. "You're taking on a bit, aren't you? It was only a remark, I made." He looked closely at Masters. "You're jumpy about something. You don't reckon to get the willies about a murder investigation. What's up? Something sinister about this party?"

Masters at last started to rub a palmful of Warlock Flake for his pipe. "Yes, there's something I don't like about it."

"Why? What sort of case is it?"

"You were quite right when you said that the victim, Frederick Hardy, was a fairly wealthy man. I say you're right because I cannot possibly understand why the local police should mention the fact unless it was significant."

"Ah! Now I see why you're so touchy. You're frightened this may turn out to be some sort of a corruption case, and that wouldn't suit you at all."

"It certainly wouldn't. I don't like corruption in the first place. It's bad enough when only money is involved, but when it starts leading to murder, it reduces this country to the level of a South American republic. Besides that, I don't think you and I would be much at home with figures. I've no desire to do the fraud squad out of a job."

"Now you're giving me the jim-jams. What're we heading into? A hot-bed of back-handers?"

Masters ignored this question. Instead he continued to give reasons for his disquiet.

"This chap died soon after he'd eaten lunch on Sunday. Apparently he liked his food."

"I know the type. Four meat meals a day and a bit of supper."

Berger laughed and then tried to stifle it. Green

said: "Let it come, lad. Don't stint yourself, or me. I don't get so much approbation that I don't like to hear it. Loosen up, son. This car's a confessional. What goes on inside it is strictly confidential, but that doesn't mean you can't behave naturally. If you've anything to add to the conversation, add it. And if you've anything to ask, ask it."

"Right, sir."

Masters approved of Green's handling of Berger, but he pushed on. "Hardy's doctor had told him to cut back on the food, so he was only indulging in—for him—a fairly light lunch. A green salad with ham and sautéed potatoes, followed by ice cream with a flaky chocolate bar crumbled over it."

"That was cutting down?"

"Apparently."

"No wonder he snuffed it. If that was a restricted diet what was his gut like? I take it he died as a direct result of the food?"

Masters grinned. "It seems inevitable, doesn't it? Yes, he died of gut's ache."

"Literally?"

"So I'm informed."

"Then what the hell are we on our way out there for?"

"Induced gut's ache?" asked Berger quietly.

"Bang on," said Masters warmly, which caused Berger to redden with pleasure. "Induced by a substance known as croton oil according to the pathologist."

"Never heard of it," said Green glumly. "And how the hell did he manage to take it in the first place?"

Masters lit his pipe. "I hadn't heard of it either, until the A.C. mentioned it this morning." He drew strongly to get the pipe glowing. "That's why I asked you to wait for a few minutes, so that I could look it up."

"And?" asked Green.

They were taking the Brentwood by-pass and heading towards Chelmsford. Here the road was much emptier, and Reed had his foot down. But this did not prevent him from making a suggestion. "Oil, you said, Chief? And this chap was eating salad? Well, salad and oil go together, don't they?"

"Quite right," replied Masters. He turned to Green.

"We've got a bright pair here."

"So sharp they'll cut themselves if they don't watch out."

"Reed's association of ideas marches with the pathologist's guess."

"Guess?"

"He can't be specific. The croton oil was found in the stomach, and as it acts quickly, it has to be assumed the oil was ingested at lunch-time. Certainly not before, and Hardy took nothing but a cup of black coffee after his ice cream. He was dead ten minutes later. The Limpid police also established that Hardy was one of those characters who didn't take mayonnaise or salad cream, but mixed his own dressing in a tablespoon, at the table, from salad oil and vinegar."

Green grimaced. "He would do. And I suppose his missus and anybody else who was eating with him contented themselves with a dollop of ready made dressing from a bottle and so are alive to tell the tale."

"You're being sharp, too."

"Give over. If only one person at a table is poisoned, it means he had something different from the others. Knowing that's not being sharp."

"But the next question is?"

"It's the obvious one. Salad oil is upstage olive oil, isn't it? Sort of super refined? There's not a lot of taste to it. So how could anybody substitute croton oil for salad oil, unless it's tasteless, too, and looks the same colour?"

"According to the book, the only taste there is to croton oil is, and I quote, 'a mild oily taste'."

"Which, mixed with vinegar, would be no different from salad oil, I suppose?"

"That's my belief. Otherwise, as you so rightly pointed out, how could it be disguised well enough to make him accept it and take it as salad oil?"

"Colour?"

"Virtually none. If mixed with salad oil it wouldn't be noticed."

"Mixed with salad oil. You mean he didn't take it neat?"

"He may have done for all I know. Certainly he must have taken a good dose because he died quickly. But from what I read about it, it is a violent substance."

"Violent is the right word if it knocks 'em off like flies. Tell us about it."

"Chapter and verse?"

"Why not? We've got nothing else to do."

"Croton oil comes from croton seeds and they, in turn, come from a small tree called *Croton Tiglium*."

"Grown in this country?"

"No. But just about everywhere else. No, that's wrong. I think they grow mostly in hot countries: India, Africa, South America, Java and such places.

The trees and seeds differ in size, form and colouring according to where they're grown, much the same as any other plants."

"Anything else in your book?"

"The seeds have a dull, cinnamon-brown colour and readily lose their caruncles."

"Their what?"

"Those little half moon bits at the end," said Berger. "You see them on broad beans."

"That's nice to know. Is it relevant?"

"You did say there was nothing else to do."

"So I did."

"The seeds contain about fifty per cent of fixed oil which contains croton-resin and crotin. I think this last is the killer as it contains croton-globulin and croton-albumin. But that's immaterial."

"Okay. How does it work?"

"You remember you started talking about gut's ache. Well, basically, croton oil is a violent cathartic, and before you ask what a cathartic is, I'll tell you it's a purge: a drug or substance that produces active bowel movements."

"Splits you open like an overdose of salts, you mean?"

"You put it so nicely! But the oil is a bit more than that. One book says the oil readily produces vesication, which means it blisters the flesh—outside or internally. Another says it raises pustules which, as you well know, are bumps or blains or whatever. A third expert refers to it as an escharotic or corrosive. In other words this bloke says it burns and chars like fire or caustic."

"Why can't they make up their minds?"

Masters tapped out his pipe in the ash tray on the

back of the driver's seat. After a moment, he said slowly: "Because croton oil is rarely, if ever, made now. The local police spent all yesterday organising a search for the possible source of the poison—and when I say possible, I don't mean probable. I mean *any* source. A general, country-wide call went out, and every pharmacy in the country was visited by their local policemen. No chemist had any. Nor did any doctor who does his own dispensing, and the drug wholesalers all said they had no stocks of it."

"What does that leave?"

"Every hospital dispensary is being asked if they have croton oil today. The only other sources I can think of are that somebody has imported it—slipped it past customs—or alternatively that somebody has got hold of the croton seeds and extracted the oil themselves."

"Oh no! Not like that ricin business?"

"It's a possibility. In that case, remember, the ricin was made into tablets. Here only the expressed oil was used. Much simpler. You could do it with a woodworking vice if you'd got the seeds."

"Here we go again. I can see now why you're tetchy about his business. An untraceable source or a chemical nightmare! Give me a good old blunt-instrument killing or a shooting or something like that. I like to get to grips with the method used: to recognise it. Here, all we've got is a violent cathartic." He stopped suddenly, and then asked, "Why should a purge kill anybody? Wouldn't it clear itself out at the same time as it cleared everything else?"

"Leaving the victim swept and garnished, you mean?"

"That's what people take all these brews for, isn't

it? Senna tea, brimstone and treacle, Epsom, Glauber and Rochelle salts and what not?"

"I've told you that croton oil readily produces blisters even on the skin. Think what would happen to your insides if you took it."

"Like swallowing a dose of mustard gas."

"Quite. Doesn't that answer the question of why croton oil can kill? Listen, and I'll tell you something else I read about it. Croton oil used to appear in the British Pharmacopoeia. Do you know what that is, Berger?"

"List of all the drugs for human consumption, sir."

"Right. But the last time croton oil was listed was in 1914—over sixty years ago. It was removed because it was so dangerous, although until then it had been an official medicine for catharsis. But the book said that even before that time, medical students who were testing the seeds—evidently testing such things was part of the identification of drugs course in those days—were warned to take the smallest possible fragment that could be cut by scalpel from a seed and to insert it on the tongue for a maximum of thirty seconds. Remember that. A pin-head size piece for a maximum of thirty seconds. Up to that time they might only notice the mild oily taste I mentioned earlier, but the book went on to state that if this warning was disregarded, considerable pain would be suffered."

"Sounds drastic enough to purge an elephant," groaned Green. "Please remind me to watch what I eat when I'm in Limpid. Oh, and remind me to wash my hands every time I go near Mr Frederick Hardy's house."

Green sat still for a moment, and then he suddenly sat up and looked across at Masters. "Hey!"

Masters grinned. "Has the penny dropped?"

"Sharp, are we? We sit here asking how he got the oil and why the pathologist wasn't sure if he'd taken it in the dressing, when all anybody had to do to get proof was to look in the salad oil bottle."

Masters, still grinning, nodded.

"Absolutely true. But you see, Greeny, by the time the local bobbies arrived on the scene—after Hardy's G.P. had called in—the oil and vinegar bottles had disappeared."

"They'd what?"

"Disappeared. Gone. Vamoosed. Mrs Hardy helped her husband from the dining room to the sitting room couch where he died almost immediately. Meanwhile the dining room had been unattended and, as it was a warm day, all the doors and windows were open."

"So somebody strolls in and nicks the evidence."

"We must assume so."

"Suffering cats! No wonder you're feeling a bit off over this one. Nobody has any idea who did the burglary? No! Don't answer that one. I only hope that whoever did pinch the bottles got some of the bloody oil on their fingers and then licked them."

"I'm sure that didn't happen, otherwise we should have heard another harrowing tale of suffering and the job would be just too easy to solve."

"What sort of suffering, sir?" asked Berger. "What I mean is, what happens if somebody takes a non-lethal dose of croton oil—like licking a greasy finger."

"The symptoms? To the best of my memory, they

are listed as intense pain in the abdomen, vomiting, purging, watery stools—"

"That's the trots," interposed Green.

"—pinched face, small and thready pulse, moist skin, and a few other things I can't remember. The treatment made me laugh, slightly, as the first instruction is stomach evacuation. I'd have thought the oil itself would have done that. Thereafter you give demulcent drinks, morphine and apply poultices to the abdomen."

"What's the time?" asked Green.

"Ten to one. Why?"

"I feel like a demulcent drink myself. That's if demulcent means what I think it does."

"It does. Soothing, mollifying, like a heady pint of draught bitter, cooled to perfection."

"Stop it," groaned Green.

"My description, or the car?"

"Your description now, the car at the next pub. I could do with a ploughman's bite, too."

"Earlier today you invited me to drink at your expense this lunchtime. Does the offer still hold or are you about to plead that circumstances alter cases?"

Green looked at him for a moment.

"Did you think I would?"

"No. But I thought you should be given the chance to renege if you felt that now was not an appropriate time."

"Then I will renege. I'd prefer to be able to savour it for more time than we've got now. How about this evening?"

"Couldn't be better."

The car slowed, and Reed drew the car up on the gravelled forecourt of a country pub.

* * *

An hour and a quarter later, Berger who was now driving said: "Limpid one mile, sir."

"Thank you. We'll go in slowly. I'd like to see what I can."

Reed said: "The gazetteer says it's a thriving old market town that originally came into prominence because of the wool trade. There's a moot hall, a guildhall, two churches—one a fourteenth century abbey foundation, the other late Georgian—the remains of the abbey and numerous other old buildings of note among which are the Victorian Corn Exchange, the town hall once used for local assizes, three old inns. . . ."

"Don't go on," said Green. "We get the picture. It's old. I'll bet by now it's ruined by supermarkets and high rise council flats."

It wasn't. Limpid was a backwater. Too far out for London overspill or commuters, and too far off the motorway routes to attract casual trade, it had not changed basically since the original mud tracks were surfaced into tarmac roads. Along the last half mile into the town centre, Masters did not see one new building. There was a short terrace of Victorian houses at one point, and nearer the market place, one or two of the shop fronts had been renewed. But at least there was nothing garish to spoil the overall effect of Limpid.

"Where to, sir?"

"The police station, please."

"Where's that, sir?"

"I really don't know, but there is a gentleman approaching us, up ahead. Yes, the one with the limp.

He looks as if he might be able to give reasonable directions."

The car drew up alongside Richard Benson.

"Excuse me, sir." Reed spoke through the open window. "Could you tell me where the police station is, please?"

"Certainly. Straight ahead. Climb the market hill—no need to tell you to keep to the left, I suppose—then turn left at the church. That is the High Street. About a hundred yards along on the left is Woolworth's. With me so far?"

"Yes, sir."

"Three or four premises past Woolworth's is a small turning left marked with a capital P for Parking sign. Take that road, pass the car park, and on the next corner is the police station. It sounds complicated, but you're not much more than a quarter of a mile away from your objective."

"Thank you, sir."

Richard Benson stood back and raised his hat courteously. But as the car drew away he stood staring after it for a moment or two. During this pause he appeared to change his mind as to his own objective, because he began to return the way he had come.

In the car, Masters said, "A very pleasant-voiced and cultured gentleman you spoke to, Reed."

"Yes, sir."

"If you look in the rear view mirror, you will see that the encounter with us seems to have caused him to change his mind. He's coming back this way—after a brief pause to consider the matter."

"So he is," said Green. "D'you reckon he knows who we are?"

"Four dirty great herbs like us in a Rover, asking for the Cop Shop? It doesn't take much figuring out, does it?"

"No. But what's his interest in us? Just nosey-parkering? Coming back to the shopping centre to tell people he's spoken to us?"

"I think not. He neither looked nor sounded like a man who would be particularly impressed by meeting a Yard team, nor did he suggest to me that he would involve himself in street corner gossip." ·

"So what is your explanation?"

"I haven't one."

By this time, Richard Benson and the car were no longer intervisible. What Masters did not know was that this day, being the first Tuesday in the month, would normally have been sale day in the Corn Exchange. Because of Hardy's sudden death, his partners had cancelled it. This had left Benson somewhat at a loose end. He had reckoned to spend most of the day at the auction, and there were a couple of items listed he would have liked to have viewed yesterday with the prospect of bidding today. But since the news of Hardy's death and—according to rumour—the manner of it, he had been thinking hard. There were some unformed ideas at the back of his mind asking to be brought out and examined quite carefully. His mind had been trying to do this as he walked in the pleasant spring sunshine. He had not picked his route consciously. His feet had carried him that way. But his encounter with the policemen—he was sure they were policemen because not only had they enquired the way to the station, but he had recognised the face of the big man sitting in the off-side back seat as the one who had appeared on television recently to answer some rather pathetic questions on the rising number of unsolved crimes—had brought him to his senses with a jolt. On sale days he always took the same route to the Corn Exchange, and as this led past the dairy he always bought meringues for tea. Events had driven them from his mind today, and he wasn't going to the Corn Exchange, but he felt he couldn't disappoint Mrs Taylor. She regarded the meringues as an expected treat. But if he was to make sure of getting them now he had remembered, he would have to return to the market hill immediately.

Berger followed the directions he had been given, and a minute or two later was braking at the kerb in front of the red brick police station. As Masters thanked him, he asked if he should come inside with them.

"Laddie," said Green, "when you're one of this team, you're on the field from kick-off to final whistle. Bung this heap round the back and then join us. You're going to hear what your job's likely to be for the next few days."

Masters led the way up the three steps and through the open door.

CHAPTER III

Chief Superintendent Telford said: "I'm pleased to meet you, Mr Masters, and all of you. But I can't say I'm pleased you're here. Quite frankly I'd have rather had our own crime squad tackle it."

Masters was struggling to keep his temper. Telford was a tall, pale man with a rectangular face and just enough hair to form an open grill across an otherwise bald pate. Head and face were the same colour—a pallor that Masters always associated with a cold sweat and clammy soft hands. The body was long and the uniform looked as if it had been cut too large. It sagged above the belt just like a badly fitting costume in a stage play. Masters objected to sloppiness in the force. Sloppiness in uniform he believed—perhaps erroneously—led to or indicated sloppiness of mind. Green was usually excruciatingly badly dressed, but his clothes were not supposed to be a smart uniform and they suited the man. Masters himself was meticulous as to dress, never feeling he could work properly if not dressed irreproachably. Telford, he thought, matched his dress to his mind—badly made up. He said he was pleased to meet them in one breath and the next said he'd prefer their absence to their presence.

"Why were we asked to come, sir?"

"The Chief Constable wanted you."

"Against your advice and wishes?"

"I felt that when a problem like this came along, our own crime squad should investigate. For two reasons. First off, they need the experience. Second, you're not going to keep men on their toes if they know that every time a plum job comes along, we're going to bring in somebody else to do it. And as a spin-off to that second reason, you're not going to get a lot out of men if they think you haven't enough confidence in them to take on a tricky job."

Masters slowly filled his pipe from the Warlock flake he had rubbed in his palm. His silence seemed to infuriate Telford.

"Well? Haven't you got anything to say about that?"

Masters looked up. "I agree with you. But before commenting, I like to hear both sides. I suppose the C.C. advanced some reason for his choice?"

Telford pinched in his mouth: a petulant grimace. "He said he thought the crime squad was better used where he had to deploy a large number of men, or for organised crime or the prevention of crime. He spouted some crap about a crime like this needing a small, specialist team that could take its time rather than a larger group which had its everyday business in the area to attend to and so might be distracted from the murder case."

"I agree with that, too. I think you have a good chance now, sir, to persuade your Chief Constable to set up a specialist squad which can be relieved of all other duties and hived off to deal with intricate emergencies. I feel sure you have people capable of dealing with the minutiae of a case such as this."

"Of course we have. They've already been working on it for forty-eight hours."

"Ah!"

"What do you mean? Ah?"

Green spoke up. "Your experience may be different, sir, but forty-eight hours is a significant figure to us at the Yard."

"I'm listening."

"We reckon that if you don't crack a case inside forty-eight hours, it's gonna be a long business."

"Oh, do you? Well all I can say to that is that I reckon we'd make as good a job of failing as you will."

Masters was lighting up. "You think the case is certain to remain unsolved, sir?"

"Look at the facts, man. We've tapped every possible source of supply of croton oil in the UK and there's been none around for years. Even the hospitals don't have it. Nil returns from everywhere. So where can you start? Then we've looked for motive. There isn't any. At least none we can discover until we find a suspect to show us in which direction to look. So, no means, no motive, and as for opportunity . . . well, you wait till you see Hardy's house, and then try to imagine what Limpid is like on a Sunday at lunchtime. It's dead. Nobody to notice anything. The Archbishop of Canterbury could have walked into that house in his full dress uniform and nobody would have noticed him."

"That sounds to me as though there was a lot of opportunity for somebody."

"For somebody. Right. But who? Dammit, we don't even know whether that somebody even came from Limpid. He might have come from Penzance for all we know."

"That thought might have occurred to your Chief Constable."

"What if it did?"

"Simply that he might have thought we might be in a better position to carry out an investigation in Penzance than would your purely parochial crime squad."

"You're taking what I said personally," accused Telford.

"Of course I am. I can understand you and your C.C. having a difference of opinion as to whether to call us in or not. But I would expect that once the decision had been taken, those differences would not be mentioned in our presence. That they have been suggests that you are still not prepared to give us your willing co-operation, even if you afford us full co-operation. I don't care for grudging help. Perhaps if you were to tell my superiors at the Yard what I have just said, they may consider my presence here unnecessary and take steps to recall me. Then we shall all be happier."

"I've heard of you, Mr. Masters, and how good you are with the words. You're good at misunderstanding, too, it seems."

"Maybe. But I am a professional and I take enormous pride in my work and achievements. I have no desire to embark on an investigation that is considered unnecessary by the people I am helping; one that is further considered to be another man's rightful perks; and finally one which is in any way likely to detract—through lack of the wholehearted confidence of my hosts—from my reputation."

"By god, if I could, I'd order you out here and now."

Telford was angry, Masters cool.

"The phone is in front of you. I'm sure your Chief Constable is available for consultation." The words were quiet, but so well spaced and enunciated that they cut the silence with almost painful, ear-piercing clarity.

Green put his pacific oar in.

"Now, now, gents! Let's not get into a tantrum about this. The thing is to get it straight. We're not here to steal anybody's thunder, Mr Telford. That's not our way. We spend our lives sorting out problems such as the one you've got here, so another one more or less is going to make no difference to us. But you ought to know that our usual way of playing it is to sort the thing out, if we can, and then leave it to the locals on whose patch it is to tie up the loose ends, make the arrests, prepare the case and so on. That means we can get away quicker to help somebody else. So it's a partnership. We play the first half, you play the second. Your boys are not going to be excluded in any way. The only thing for you to decide is whether you want to take the field for the whole of the game or only half of it."

Masters turned to his subordinate. "Thank you, Chief Inspector. I'm glad of your explanation." He turned to Telford. "I'm taking my people off now for tea. We had only a snack lunch, so we can do with it. Our absence will give you time to think. I'll be back at four o'clock to hear what you've decided."

Telford didn't reply immediately. He sat back in

his chair with his thumbs in his belt. Masters noted that the cold sweat he had expected to see on the pale face had broken out on Telford's upper lip. The Chief Superintendent eyed them for a moment or two, then leaned forward and spoke into an intercom. "Desk? Send in tea for five, sandwiches for eight—and make them good ones. Oh, and add some cakes or chocolate biscuits. As quickly as possible."

He leaned back again.

Masters said: "We appreciate the hospitality, sir."

"Dammit," said Telford explosively, leaning forward to emphasise what he was saying. "That's the sort of thing I wanted to do for you. That's why I'm here personally in Limpid to meet you. I felt I couldn't let you arrive at a Chief Inspector's station with no sign of a headquarters' recognition. I may have worded it badly, but what I've been trying to say is I've no objection to you or the Yard. Only to your being here when this case could be of such value to my own men. East Anglia isn't so full of this sort of crime that we get a chance to do our stuff very often. And I wanted my men to have this chance. Trouble is, I couldn't guarantee the Chief Constable that we'd succeed. How could I? This case is going to be a bastard for whoever takes it on. I know that. But how do I know what our squad can do if they're not allowed to try?"

"To whom would you have given the case if it had been left to you?"

"My crime squad Superintendent and a fairly bright young Inspector."

"Are they the people who have done all the spadeworks so far?"

"Yes, and they're disappointed men at this moment."

"Can you spare them and a car for the rest of the week?"

"I'd have to, wouldn't I, if you weren't here?"

Masters turned to Green. "If we borrow their car for you and Berger, will you be happy to have Mr Telford's bright young Inspector with you?"

"Like a shot. A boy with local knowledge."

"To help you. Not under instruction, although if you can give him a few tips I daresay it would be appreciated."

"Understood."

Telford had been sitting quiet, his lips slightly parted. Masters turned to him. "I'll be glad to have your Superintendent working alongside me. It's not an arrangement I've ever made before, but if you are happy with it. . . ?"

"I'm happy all right." Telford really did seem eager to accept. "And my two will be chuffed to be in with a Yard squad. It's a chance they'll take with both hands."

"Then we'll call that settled. When can we meet them?"

"You're in a hurry?"

"I don't like to give trails time to grow cold."

"They're out and about on this business now. I'll call them in. They should be here by the time we've had tea. Oh, and by the way, I've booked rooms for you at the Swan and Cygnets on the High Street."

"Thank you."

"Superintendent Wally Frimley and Inspector Colin Hoame."

Telford introduced the two newcomers and asked them to sit. He then explained the arrangements that had been made for them to collaborate with Masters' team.

Frimley spoke for both of them and expressed satisfaction at the thought of working alongside the Yard, and with this team in particular.

Masters, like most other people, enjoyed hearing a little praise, but he hurriedly asked Frimley to tell them what his people had been doing since they took over the case on Sunday.

"Monday, really," replied Frimley. "We didn't suspect foul play until the doctors had finished their discussion and the pathologist had pronounced. What really clinched it was the disappearance of the double oil and vinegar bottle when we wanted to have its contents analysed."

"Double bottle?" asked Green. "What was it like?"

"I didn't see it, of course. But Mrs Hardy's description is that it was like two flasks put together. Pear shaped flasks with one flat side each. They were joined on this flat side but the necks—or the stalks of the pears if you like to think of them that way—were elongated and curved over in opposite directions. Each mouth had a stopper, of course, but if you held the thing over your food to pour out vinegar, say, you wouldn't get oil, because the mouth of the half containing oil would be curved upwards."

"Got it," said Green. "I've seen them abroad, I think."

"Did you ask what colour the glass was?" enquired Masters.

"Smoky colour."

"So if the croton oil was slightly different in color

from the salad oil in which it was mixed, nobody would have been able to notice it."

"That's right. And after tipping a drop into a spoon and mixing it with vinegar, nobody would be able to tell the difference either."

"Fine. That settles that point. Now, having decided you'd got a murder case on your hands, what did you do?"

Hoame said: "I organised an enquiry round about to see if anybody had noticed anybody going into or out of the Hardy house. It seemed to me that if I could get a lead there, I'd be on the way to finding who had killed Hardy."

"No luck?"

"None."

"I," said Frimley, "tried to trace the source of the croton oil. I think you've heard we've enquired of every likely source in the country, again with no joy."

"That's a lot to have achieved. At any rate you've eliminated one route. Anything else?"

"Today should have been auction day. Hardy and his two partners hold an auction on the first Tuesday of every month in the Corn Exchange. Today's sale and yesterday's viewing were both cancelled because of Hardy's death, but people have been buying catalogues for the past fortnight and in case any of them had not heard of Hardy's death or that the sale had been cancelled, Hoame and I spent some time there."

"Did anybody turn up?"

"Quite a few. Fifty or sixty all told. We were able to ask a lot of questions—particularly of the regulars—in case anything was known of bad blood between Hardy and a client. Nothing specific came up, but we learned that a goodish number regarded him as a bit of a crook."

"With good reason?"

"We got no evidence."

"What about his estate agency side? Have you looked into that?"

"We've enquired at every house he's sold during the past three years. That's about forty or so. Nobody feels he sold them a pup, though one or two think his prices were too steep."

"That's inevitable these days. Is that the lot?"

"That's it."

"Thank you. It's been a frustrating job for you, and something like it will have to continue, I'm afraid."

"Such as?" asked Hoame.

Green said: "Hasn't it occurred to you, laddie, that it's not only the people Hardy sold property to, but those he sold it for who might be just a little upset if he'd gypped them?"

"How?"

"Well, what if a chap went to him and said, 'I want to sell my house for forty thousand.' Hardy—who was a valuer, I suppose—looks it over, discovers it *is* worth forty thousand, but says it's only worth thirty. He then finds a buyer at thirty—himself working through a third party. Once he's got it for thirty, he sells it for forty—again through his third party. Ten thousand nicker made on one deal. But the original owner finds out. What's his opinion of Hardy?"

"He could sue him."

"What for?"

Hoame thought for a moment and then shrugged.

"So, laddie, we've got a bit more searching to do."

Telford, who had so far sat quietly, turned to Masters. "I reckon I know what you're going to say next."

"In that case, be my guest."

"It's that bottle, isn't it?"

"You must agree that we will have to try and find an explanation for why whoever killed Hardy risked his neck to come back to the house to remove the bottle. It was risky enough the first time, coming to leave the croton-oil, so there must have been a powerful reason for removing it after the man was already dead."

Hoame said. "We hadn't got round to that."

"But we ought to have done," rejoined Frimley. "It makes me sick to think I didn't spot that." He looked across at Masters with some concern. "You're not suggesting he collected it to use it again, are you?"

"If it's a possibility, we must bear it in mind. But I would say one murderer is clever. He used a means we can't trace to its source, he timed the assault to a nicety and he had the guts to come and go at great risk to himself. If such a person was intending to kill a second person in the same way, I would say he had enough intelligence and foresight to hold some of the croton-oil back for the purpose, rather than run unnecessary risks."

"That's good thinking," approved Telford. "So you needn't get too worried about multiple murders, Wally."

Masters looked across at Hoame. "Now, D.I., leading on from what I've just said, what can you further tell us about our murderer?"

Hoame frowned in concentration.

"Come on, laddie," said Green, who had taken the

embarrassed Hoame under his wing. "The Super said this chap was intelligent and brave and what else?"

"Good at timing."

"What does that suggest?"

"That he knew exactly when the Hardys had lunch."

"What else?"

"That he must have known they were having salad for lunch."

"And?"

"And?"

"Well, he didn't kill Mrs Hardy, did he?"

"You mean he knew only Hardy himself used oil and vinegar whereas his wife ate mayonnaise?"

"You're doing a good job. So what's your conclusion?"

"Conclusion? Oh, yes! As he knows so much about the Hardys, he must be a close friend or relative."

"Great."

"Don't stop," urged Masters. "Suck it dry."

But Hoame was finished. It was Frimley who said: "He could have put the croton oil in at any time before Sunday lunch. Say on Saturday or Friday, because he didn't care when Hardy took it. . . ."

"Hey, wait a minute," interposed Telford.

Masters turned interrogatively to the Chief Superintendent.

"It had to be arranged so that Hardy would take it on Sunday, so's the murderer would know when to collect the bottle. Hadn't it?"

Masters grinned delightedly.

"You've made a good point, sir. But is it valid? Yes or no?"

Telford sat forward. "No, blast it, it isn't."

"Why not?"

"Say our murderer did put the oil in two or three days early, and then kept a watch."

"Kept watch?" asked Hoame. "How?"

"Can anybody see into the dining room with a telescope for instance? If so, he'd only have to watch lunch and supper for a couple of days."

"Excellent," murmured Masters. "But to get back to where we were before Mr Telford made his point—which must, incidentally, be investigated—what about Wally's line of reasoning? Berger, can you see anything in that?"

"Yes, sir, I can. Mr Frimley says the oil could have gone in at any time. So it could if whoever put it there knew Hardy's eating habits. Say he knew Hardy had lunch at a pub every working day—and Saturday is a working day for estate agents, usually—and went out to dinner at a club or somewhere on Friday nights and took his missus out on Saturday nights. Why then, sir, he'd know Sunday lunch would be the first main meal Hardy would eat at home after the oil was planted."

"So that reinforces our former theory that the killer knows the Hardys well enough to be aware of their domestic habits. Go on, somebody, please. Keep the ball rolling."

"Sir," said Reed, "one man would know for sure when the Hardys were going to have salad. The greengrocer. If Mrs Hardy went in on Saturday morning and bought lettuce and tomatoes and so on and said, as most women do, that she wanted everything very fresh because it had to keep till Sunday, he'd know her plans."

"Excellent. Anything else?"

This time nobody leapt in with an idea. Masters, however, was not prepared to stop yet.

"When Mr Telford told me he knew what I was going to say next, he was quite right. The bottle was the next item on my list, but I hadn't quite finished the previous point. Mr Green has very rightly pointed out—and I use his word—that Hardy may have gypped somebody over selling a property of the real estate variety, as the Americans call it. But let us not forget that he sells—or auctions—other things—which may be of considerable value. I think I'd be right in saying that the antique world offers tremendous scope for faking, wrong describing, underselling, overpricing and so on and so forth. It's a world I know little about, and I may be doing most people with those interests a great injustice, but an unscrupulous man is an unscrupulous man in any walk of life. So we shall have to look very carefully at what his firm has auctioned for some time back, and that is going to be a bit of a routine chore."

He turned to Telford. "In your brief to the Yard, sir, you made the point that Hardy was a wealthy man. Why mention that particularly?"

"I also said he was a town councillor. Both points seemed relevant to me. But I suppose really it was because I was surprised at the extent of his interests and the size of his investments. Of course I don't know everything. I looked into that side of his affairs myself—interviewed his solicitor, accountant and bank manager. But the fact is, I've been around these parts for a good many years now, and I've known of Hardy for a long time. It isn't all that long ago that he didn't have all that much money. And when a small town estate agent gathers a lot of money in a very short time and he is then murdered, it seems relevant to me. As a possible clue as to a line of enquiry, I mean. Not as a special reason for doing more to find his murderer than, say, the killer of a tramp."

"It does give us another line to consider. Thank you." He addressed them all. "Well, gentlemen, that is all for this session. What we have discussed we will sleep on and then start to follow up tomorrow."

"Nothing more tonight?" asked Frimley.

"You and Hoame have had a couple of tiring days and it's now after five o'clock. My people and I want to settle in at our pub. But above all, I want you to think about what we've discussed and to cast around in your minds for other points and other avenues for investigation. The basis for the successful conclusion of many crimes is routine work—when there are woods to search and house to house enquiries to make. But for a crime such as this which will need thought rather than legwork, then thought it must be."

Telford stood up.

"Mr Masters, I want to thank you. My boys and I have had an eye-opener. You've seen nobody connected with this crime, haven't visited the scene, had no dabs or photographs or other material evidence offered to you, but yet you've been able, in the space of an hour or so, to take us quite a long way along the road of how to tackle the problem. And when I say take us, I mean just that. You've made us do the thinking and shown us how to view things. It was a professional job, and I'm pleased to have seen you in action."

"That's right enough," added Frimley. "Do you always work like this?"

"Not quite so formally perhaps, but we brainstorm in the car, and we do what I've asked everybody here to do tonight—think and think widely—laterally as well as vertically. But the big thing in this sort of exercise is never to be afraid of your own ideas—lest they might be stupid—and never to laugh at anybody else's ideas. Ideas beget ideas in your own heads as well as in a group like this."

They were all now on their feet.

Telford took Masters aside. "I'm going back to HQ now. I was going to stay over to see how things went. I don't think I need bother after this. But I'd be grateful if you could keep me informed on your progress."

"I'll do that if you want me too, of course. But let Frimley and Hoame make the daily reports to you. It will give them a greater feeling of involvement."

"You're right at that. But I'll come over to see you, just the same."

Before they left the station, Masters told Reed to pick up a street map of Limpid from the desk sergeant and to get from him the address and phone number of Hardy's home and office. As Masters and Green were getting into the car, Reed caught them up. "Here you are, Chief. I've got the phone number of the nick and the pub as well, and I've marked all the places on the map."

As they drew out of the station yard, Masters said quietly: "Thanks, Greeny."

"What for?"

"Putting the quieteners in. Neither of us could have backed down very gracefully if you hadn't spoken."

"You treated old Telford very well after that."

"Because he gave me an explanation with which I had some sympathy and which I was able to take as an apology."

"But that show you put on to baffle him! Talk about pulling the wool."

"I had to do something by way of reparation, and I could see they were floundering. They'd worked hard, but they hadn't thought about what to do and how to do it. So, if we could give them a free lesson and fly the flag for the Yard, why not? It didn't do them any harm, did it?"

Berger, who was driving, said without looking round. "It helped me, sir. A real eye-opener, I found it. I could feel myself starting to think. I'd been thinking before, but mostly that I couldn't see where on earth you were going to begin on a case like this. I couldn't see an obvious starting point."

Green shrugged his shoulders. "There's your answer, George. And there's the Swan and Cygnets. How about a dirty great pint of wallop on me before we do anything else?"

"Why on you, Mr Green?" asked Reed.

"You mean you don't know?" asked Green, slightly affronted.

"The Yard grapevine didn't have time to work before we left," said Masters. "Detective Inspector Green is now Detective Chief Inspector Green, and we are privileged in being present to help him celebrate the promotion."

Berger drove the car carefully down the narrow garage entrance of the Swan and Cygnets and pulled up in the yard behind. "This do, sir?"

"For the time being."

As they dismounted, Green said: "Are you thinking of going out again tonight?"

"After dinner. You and I. I don't mind letting the locals in on some of our trade secrets, but not all of them. We're not here solely as a training cadre, you know."

"I might have known it. Where are we going?"

"First off, to see Hardy's widow. After that, I don't quite know."

"But you've got a plan?"

"Shall we call it an idea."

Masters watched Berger and Reed disappear into the inn with the bags and then added. "It's to do with that salad oil bottle."

"What about it?"

"Why do you think the murderer took the risk he did in removing it?"

"That's easy. There was something incriminating about it. All that about wanting it for a second murder was so much crap."

"Why should it be incriminating?"

"Lord knows, unless he realised he'd left his dabs on it."

"That's a possibility, I suppose."

"But you don't reckon so?"

"Let me ask you this. What if it were a substitute bottle?"

"I don't get you."

"What if it wasn't Hardy's bottle, but one very like it."

"Yet different enough for somebody to tell them apart?"

"Yes."

"Who?"

"The daily woman, perhaps, who washes up the bottle. Don't you grow accustomed to your household things—size, shape, colour, weight and so on? So accustomed, in fact, that if somebody was to substitute something of yours with another item that was very similar, you would immediately spot the difference?"

"Come to think of it. . . ."

"Yes?"

"You're right. You're bloody right, like you always are. It stands to reason the murderer wouldn't walk into Hardy's house with his croton oil in a medicine bottle and stand there decanting it into a curved neck. His hands would be shaking so much he'd never hit the hole, and he'd spill the stuff on his own hands. Don't forget it blisters skin. And he certainly couldn't do it wearing gloves. So he had to find a similar bottle, prime it with croton and salad oil on one side and vinegar on the other, and then come and substitute it."

"Right. But he knew the bottles weren't quite the same in some respect, so he had to whip his bottle away again, because it could be traced back to him."

"But why not put Hardy's bottle back again?"

"Good point. We'll have to think about that one."

They entered the inn and signed the book.

"So it's a quick wash, a quick pint, an early dinner and a visit to Mrs Hardy, is it?"

"I think so, don't you?"

Unusually for him, Masters was driving. Green, who disliked the front of a car and would never sit on the offside if he could help it, sat in the rear nearside corner and navigated from the street map.

Earlier, it had been suggested that Hardy's house

was isolated, but Masters had not realised quite what this meant. He had envisaged wide open spaces, but Pellucid House was in the centre of the town, barely two hundred yards from the market place. Green, nevertheless, had some difficulty with his directions.

Limpid was, basically, a crossroads. There were, of course, scores of other roads and lanes within the huddled little town, but they were merely capillaries running from the main arteries to serve the various parts of the urban body.

Pellucid House lay in the south east quadrant of the town, to the right of the road by which the Yard men had entered the town that afternoon: off somewhere opposite the spot where they had stopped and enquired the way of Benson. But there was no road leading to it from there, merely a sort of wide alley, wide enough—just—to take a car. As there was over a hundred yards of this lane, running between the side walls of houses facing the main road, then past the fronts of cottages, and finally between garden walls, with no sign of a gate, to the Pellucid House grounds, Masters stopped short.

"Is this marked as a road?"

"Yes."

"Is there another way to it?"

There was. Green showed him the map. If they were to retrace their route and then, instead of turning left, as formerly, at the High Street, they were to turn right for a hundred yards, they would come to another minor road on the right. This seemed to be as far away from Pellucid House as the road they were now on. But a track similar to the one that now faced them led from this minor road. The map showed it as a double dotted line, which led at right angles from the minor road, divided into a circle to enclose the Pellucid House grounds, and then came together again to form the track that Masters had refrained from taking.

"Shove it into the side and walk," suggested Green.

Masters accepted the advice. He parked the car and they trudged up the lane. As they approached the end of the straight portion where the circle began, the walls of the Pellucid House garden stood up eight feet before them. But it wasn't a straight wall. It was a wavy one, scalloped along its length in a wavy line. Green paused and looked at Masters. "This is a new one on me."

"You find it sometimes. The waves turn the wall through the points of the compass, so that you get east, west or south facing areas every eight or ten feet. You grow whatever needs heat and therefore suits south facing walls on the south bits, things that like a good deal of shade on the east facing bits, and those that like a lot of light on the west facing bits. A further advantage is that you get a lot more wall this way than you would by enclosing the same area with straight walls. That means you can grow more morello cherries or apricots or whatever."

"Intensive culture?"

"You could call it that. Now, right or left?"

"I'll opt for left."

"So be it."

Green was correct. They came to the main gate after travelling a quarter of the circle. The house was off-centre in its grounds. Had they gone the other way they would have come to a garden gate giving to a pathway to the back of the house.

Maud Hardy was not alone. As she ushered them

into the drawing room, Masters saw that two other women were already seated there. As Mrs Hardy introduced them—a Mrs Horbium and a Mrs Wellerby—Masters thought that he could not have found three more dissimilar women to bring together had he tried. Mrs Hardy was very tall and skinny. Her bones stood out in all visible places—on her face, at her elbows, wrists and knuckles—and her legs were painfully thin. She was a faded woman. Never a beauty, he would have guessed, and never one with a figure. Green, who liked well-covered women, would be mentally cataloguing her as like two boards clapped together. But she was expensively dressed. The short-sleeved cotton frock she wore was not the sort a working girl would have been able to afford. Masters felt it was unsuitable—not because of her bereavement, but because of her age. The necklet was gold, if he was any judge. So was the heavy bracelet, while eternity rings such as the one she wore were not bought two on a card for 25 pence.

Mrs Horbium, who had stood up with a squawk of surprise when Masters was introduced as being from the Yard, was squat and stout. He estimated her hip measurement to be twice his own—what Green would describe as built for comfortable sitting, and with a centre of gravity as low as that of a Kelly doll. Mrs Horbium was in black: a black dress with flounces intended to hide some of her girth, but only serving to emphasise her outrageous proportions. She had long, pendant jade earrings and a blue rinse, green fingernails and high heeled court shoes too small for her fat feet. She also wore too much face powder.

Mrs Wellerby was different. She was an attractive woman in her mid-thirties, attractively dressed in a tan moygashel suit, sheer nylons on excellent legs, and low-heeled tan shoes. Her hair was fair, straight and long, her face unwrinkled and her eyes bright. She looked, to Masters, wholesome, charming and intelligent. He liked the feel of her cool fingers as they shook hands.

Mrs Horbium said, in a kittenish voice that jarred the nerves and made Masters cringe inwardly, "But how thrilling to be actually here when Scotland Yard called! We all heard that you were coming to Limpid, of course, but we had no idea you would wish to interview us so soon. I've never been questioned by the police before but I find myself quite looking forward to it."

"Grace," said Mrs Wellerby, "I think you've got hold of the tarry end of the stick. These gentlemen are here to see Mrs Hardy, not us. We'd better leave."

"Unless," said Green, "there is some reason why Mrs Horbium thinks she ought to be questioned."

The young woman flushed at Green's tone. "Oh, I'm sure there isn't."

"Mrs Horbium obviously expected us to interview her. Perhaps you would care to tell us why, Mrs Horbium."

"Dear me, I thought you would be talking to everybody in Limpid. I mean, nobody knows who poisoned Mr Hardy, do they? So you'll have to investigate us all to find clues and things, won't you?"

"I hope not, ma'am." Green sounded resigned: as if he were saying that he'd met some loonies in his time, but Mrs Horbium took the biscuit.

Maud Hardy said in a colourless voice, "Grace, dear, you'll have to excuse me now. It was very nice of you to come, and you, too, Joanna."

Masters exclaimed aloud, "Joanna Wellerby! Of course! I was wondering where I'd seen your face before. You're the pianist, I believe, ma'am."

"One of them, at any rate." The smile for Masters was warm and friendly.

"I have actually attended concerts at which you've played," said Masters, "so I should have known you immediately."

"I expect when you see a vaguely familiar face you mentally flick through the rogues' gallery, looking for it. You probably don't think, at first, to include solo instrumentalists in the mental identity parade."

"I shall make a note to do so in future."

She turned to her companion. "Come along, Grace. We're out-staying our usefulness if not our welcome. Goodbye, Mrs Hardy. Perhaps you will let me come again some time."

While Mrs Hardy saw her guests out, Masters looked round the room. It was, he guessed, the better part of forty feet long and eighteen or twenty wide. A magnificent room, and even more important to Masters, magnificently furnished. Even Green was impressed, and he was not one usually to enthuse about fine pieces of period furniture.

"This must have cost him a bomb."

"I wonder," murmured Masters.

"Why, some of this stuff must be worth a mint. Look at it. That sideboard thing. . . ."

"Chiffonier."

"If you say so; and this swivel-topped games table. I've seen things like this on the telly and they cost more than I'd use for furnishing a whole house."

"You're quite right about their value. I was merely questioning whether Hardy had paid the market price for them or even, wealthy though he is, whether he could afford to."

"How d'you mean?"

"A collection such as this, especially if it is repeated in every room in the house, would take a lifetime to collect. Or even generations. But our information is that Hardy became wealthy only comparatively recently. On the other hand, he is an auctioneer, and so is, as it were, constantly handling such items.

"You're saying he fiddled it somehow?"

"It's a possibility."

"It's a certainty, and you know it."

Masters wandered round inspecting the room's contents until Mrs Hardy returned.

"We're very sorry to intrude upon you, Mrs Hardy, but you will appreciate that we must do our best to get on the trail of whoever poisoned your husband as quickly as possible."

"I understand." She sat in an embroidered armchair which Masters judged, from the curved front crinoline stretcher, to be of the Queen Anne period. "What do you want to know?" She had not invited them to sit, and Masters made no move to do so. Green was restless, and Masters could guess why. Green wasn't over-blessed with good manners himself, but he had come to expect the courtesies in others, particularly in people who lived in houses such as this. When he didn't find what he expected he grew fidgety—mentally as well as physically.

"Just for the moment, Mrs Hardy, I would like to talk about your double oil and vinegar bottle. Do you happen to know its provenance."

"Its what?"

"Where it came from, who made it and so on."

"Oh, I can tell you that. Fred bought a sideboard with a few things in it about two years ago, and the bottle was in it. I didn't know what it was, but he did, being in the trade, like, and he said: 'Maud, this is for oil and vinegar.' Until then he'd always had Heinz like me, but from then on, he never used anything but oil and vinegar. Fancied himself mixing French dressing in a spoon, I reckoned, particularly when we had company." She finished her listless recital and then looked up at Masters and uttered a single word: "Why?"

Masters ignored the question. "Can you describe its colour exactly?"

"It wasn't very nice. Crude. I thought it was. It was neither yellow nor green. Bit of both I dare say. Looked as if it had been made out of old beer bottles."

"Were there any marks in the glass?"

"On the bottom, you mean? I didn't notice. I don't wash up, you know." It was a rebuke.

"I didn't mean a maker's name. I meant flaws or flecks. You said it was crude. What made it crude?"

"Well . . . what I meant was we could have had a nice cut-glass cruet. One of those with five bottles on a silver stand. Much nicer, it would have been."

"Of course. But the double bottle your husband chose to use—he must have had a high opinion of it, otherwise he wouldn't have gone against your wishes by having it on the table, would he?"

"Oh, he thought it was something—I don't quite know what."

"But you can't remember any distinguishing marks."

"Oh, yes I can. It was such poor glass, there were flecks in it. White ones—dirty white, really. It made it look quite low class."

"Were they in any particular part of the glass."

"Mostly in the bulb part on the oil side. There was a sort of half-moon of them in one place. About half as big as an old sixpence."

"That seems very clear. Did you see the half-moon on Sunday?"

"I didn't notice."

"I see. What were the stoppers like?"

"Corks, with dull old pewter tops."

"I see. Thank you. Are you alone in the house?"

"My daily is sleeping here at the moment."

"No living-in maids?"

"These days?"

"My information is that you have had this house for about six years. Isn't it a big place to have bought for just two people getting on in years?"

"My husband called it his insurance policy."

"Meaning he proposed to sell it?"

"When he got the right buyer, yes."

"Thank you." Masters turned to Green and raised his eyebrows interrogatively.

Green asked: "Was the back gate always kept locked and bolted, Mrs Hardy?"

"Oh no, that was the tradesman's entrance. How would they have got in if the gate was always bolted?"

"In that case," said Green, "do you mind if we go out that way?"

"If you like. Through the conservatory."

It was almost a dismissal, but Masters had one more question. "Is there somebody in Limpid who is very knowledgeable about antiques?"

"Mrs Horbium."

"Really?"

"But Mr Benson is the real clever one."

"Mr Benson? Could you, by any chance, tell me where he lives?"

"Oh yes. Dicky Benson lives in a flat above the shops at the corner of the High Street. Over the greengrocer's and the leather shop. The door's in between."

"Thank you. We'll take advantage of your offer now, and go out through the conservatory."

She showed them the way. They followed the flagged path, but, as Green pointed out, anybody could have reached the house unseen by sticking to the bushes and trees.

Masters agreed. When they reached the car he said: "I'm going to try and find this Benson chap. Are you coming with me?"

CHAPTER IV

By now the little town was quiet. It was half past nine, and not yet time for the pubs to empty, so there were very few people on the streets. A few cars were parked on the market square and a cinema front glowed not far away. Probably the cars belonged to members of the sparse audience.

"Not even any courting couples under the lamp-lights," said Green.

"That's no longer the fashion."

"What isn't? Courting or standing under lamps?"

"Both, I suppose. The telly has put an end to both. Nobody goes courting nowadays. They have ninepen-north of. hot hand watching *Kojak* these days. It's no longer 'walking out together' like it used to be."

Masters parked the car just after turning into the High Street. The shops he was looking for were just behind them on the left. They walked back looking for the entrance to Benson's flat. They found it easily enough: a narrow, white-painted door, separating the front of the greengrocer's premises from those of the leather merchant. The bell was of the push-button type, set in a large, concave, brass finger plate. Masters put his thumb on it decisively.

Almost immediately an outside light went on above his head, and another came on inside the building, as the fanlight above the door showed. There was, however, an appreciable pause before he heard bolts being drawn, a deadlock turned and a spring lock being unbuttoned. Even then, the door, when it opened, was held by a chain.

The light on both sides of the door was good enough for mutual recognition. Masters was sufficiently taken aback to pause for a significant moment or so before he asked: "Mr Richard Benson?"

"I am he. I believe we have met before. This afternoon. I guessed then you were a policeman."

"I am a policeman. Superintendent Masters and my colleague, Detective Chief Inspector Green, both of Scotland Yard."

"I presume you wish to speak to me, otherwise there could be no point in your calling at this time of night. You had better come in." The chain was withdrawn and the door opened wide with unstinting welcome, but Masters noticed that Benson, still armed with his ashplant, gripped it firmly. Such preparedness for action, Masters decided charitably, was more a result of habit than peculiar to this single visit.

"I will go first," said Benson as he closed the door on the deadlock only. "And you will bear with me, I trust, if I am a little slow on the stairs. I have a stiff knee."

"War wound?" asked Green as Benson started up the close-carpeted flight.

"You could almost call it that," agreed Benson as he swung his right leg up a riser. "But not in the accepted sense that the wound was received during hostilities with a declared enemy. No, I came through the main struggle relatively unscathed."

Masters, coming last, was looking about him. The stairs rose out of a tiny hall which led nowhere, but merely provided a certain amount of base to the stairwell, preventing the flight from being forced to rise claustrophobically between two walls set no further apart than its own width. He could see the reason for the stair light, too. Without it, even in daytime, the flight would be dark, for apart from the fanlight at the front door there was no other direct light. Perhaps that was why Benson had had it decorated white. Everything dead white, even the close-piled carpet which 'gave' under every footstep, but yet remained firm to the tread to emphasise that it had been expensively made and well laid.

"Some minor shindig?" asked Green.

"I was in the government service," admitted Benson. "There was trouble in the country to which I was accredited. The house was attacked one night."

"I see."

Benson had stopped at the top, where the stairs pierced the back wall of the hall. Here the opening was only as wide as the stairs and it was here—strategically placed—that a wrought iron gate faced them. It stretched from the top riser to the ceiling. The sort of installation one might find either in a garden or, alternatively, in a bank.

"I never carry the key to this on my person," explained Benson, putting his arm between two of the metal uprights. "I hang it out of sight, round the corner, just within reach. I trust that being out of sight, it will be out of mind should anybody attempt a break-in."

"Very wise," murmured Green. "And a tea-leaf wouldn't find the key on your person if he broke in down below and overpowered you."

"Quite." The gate swung open. Benson led the way through, leaving Masters to close it. "But I feel that on this occasion I needn't lock it—not with Scotland Yard on the premises."

Four small steps at right angles to the first flight and they were in the flat proper.

The place was softly lit with reading lamps. Masters paused to appreciate it.

"It is a quaint place," said Benson, seeing Masters taking in his surroundings. "I call this my hall. Achieved by the simple expedient of removing the wall of one room and so leaving a goodly empty space at the head of the stairs. But the apartment spans two shops of slightly different interior heights. And so my bedrooms and bathroom which lie to your right stand almost two feet above the level of my day quarters and kitchen which are to your left. My sitting room is this way."

He led the way to a door halfway down the left side of the good-sized square hall. Here, too, the decor was dead white. But inside the sitting room, the effect was different. The dominating colours were browns and reds. Brown graded from buff to horse-chestnut, and reds from crimson to the pink of the wall lights. It was an unlikely combination, but an homogenous whole. Is struck Masters that a man and a woman had each chosen to make it their room and by chance their choices had formed a happy marriage of effect. A good room, a big room, tastefully furnished. Masters liked it.

So did Green. He said: "I'd never have believed I'd ever find anything like this over a greengrocer's shop. You and your missus must have worked hard to turn it into this, sir."

"I am a widower, Mr Green. My wife was killed in the same incident in which I was wounded."

"I'm sorry to hear that. Mau-Mau job was it?"

"Something like that. Be seated, please, gentlemen. And name your personal poisons. I believe I can cater for most tastes, except the modern nasties like rum and coke."

"Honest ale," said Masters.

"And for me," added Green.

Benson busied himself at a wine cabinet and then came across with two tankards.

"Genuine leather?" asked Masters, taking his.

Benson nodded and Green said: "I never knew they made them like this. Leather tankards, eh? Cheers!" He drank deep and sighed with satisfaction before wiping his mouth with the back of his hand.

Benson smiled and turned to Masters. "I am pleased to welcome you to my home, but I hardly think this is a purely social call, is it?"

"We were given your name and address by Mrs Hardy. I asked her if Limpid boasted an antiquarian of repute and she referred me to you."

"For what purpose?" Masters thought the eyes looked slightly worried at the mention of Mrs Hardy. At any other time, he might have paid no attention to this, but coupled with what he regarded as Benson's peculiar behaviour in the afternoon, he felt it could be significant—of what, he couldn't say. Just significant.

"For some information on salad oil bottles."

"My dear sir!"

"Double bottles, Mr Benson. Crude, greeny-grey, with white flecks in the glass. Doesn't that suggest something to you?"

"Of course it does, as it obviously does to you."

"I'm guessing. Hardy treasured his bottle. They're collectors' items, aren't they?"

"Collectors' items, certainly. The early, genuine ones. But they're not particularly valuable pieces. And, of course, you can get the modern equivalents which have probably depreciated the value of them all."

"You can get the modern equivalent of a Ming vase."

"Touché. But Ming is excellent work. Salad bottles, as you call them, were crudely made originally and they're still crudely made. You can even buy them with rather unhygienic raffia stoppers on the continent."

"What should the stoppers be made of?"

"Certainly not rubber. As you know, oils attack rubber."

"So what, then?"

"Glass—if the necks were sufficiently carefully made to take a ground glass stopper. Otherwise, a silver or pewter cap made like a farthing-nail so that one could use cork and renew it when necessary simply by skewering a new one on the spindle."

"I understand that. Did you ever see Hardy's bottle."

"Never. I heard he used one for French dressing,

but Hardy and I were no more than the merest acquaintances. We were in no sense friends." Benson put down his tankard. "May I ask why you are asking these questions? I am not averse to helping you, but like most people, I like to know to what end I am working."

"You were in the government service, sir."

"Meaning I should know better than to ask inconvenient questions and I should be prepared to help unquestioningly."

"Something of the sort."

"I've been pensioned off a long time." He grinned as Green looked round the room. "No, Mr Green, it is not all provided by a government pension. I have a little money of my own. So had my wife and—a couple of years ago—her mother died shortly after her father, and as my wife was their only child, they very kindly made me a beneficiary under the will. It allows me independence and a chance to indulge my hobby. Otherwise I might have become a dealer for a living."

"You never sell?"

"I have done so. I stick, for the most part, to small objects. But occasionally I have discovered and bought a few large items because I could not resist them at the time. Later I have regretted my folly and have disposed of them—always at a profit. To have done otherwise would have been unrealistic."

Masters dragged the conversation back.

"I understand experts like to talk on their subjects. Indulge your expertise now—on salad bottles."

"You're harping on that bottle, Mr Masters."

"It contained the poison," explained Green.

"Did it? Thank you for telling me that. I surmised

it had done so. And since you are asking about it, I also presume it has disappeared and you are hoping to trace it."

Masters strove to keep his patience. "That is roughly the way of it."

"A bottle such as that could be broken and disposed of quite easily."

"The point had occurred to us, sir."

"I'm sure it had. Ah, well, persistence has its own reward, or as my old mother used to say, impudence and fortitude will get you anywhere. So here goes, gentlemen. To begin with, we will refer to the item under discussion as a flask or a twin flask, whichever you prefer. These flasks, joined together like Siamese twins, were called gimmel flasks, and their original purpose was not for holding oil and vinegar, but to allow lovers to plight their troth by drinking simultaneously from the two necks. Quite how the necks were directed in those days, I cannot say, but I would guess that instead of curving in opposite directions, they were arc-ed together, opening out in a V, so that the two young people could drink cheek to cheek.

"Interesting," said Masters. "I felt sure these things had a more romantic origin than oil and vinegar containers. Gimmel flasks! Is gimmel a corruption of gemini, meaning twins?"

"It could be. But I think that the term applies to the linking of the flasks rather than the fact that there were two of them. Perhaps that would be clearer if I were to say that I think even if there were three flasks joined together they would still be referred to as gimmel. Gemini would have no credence then."

"I see. So the origin of gimmel is . . . ?"

"I suspect from gimmal, which is an antique finger ring made so that it will divide into two or three rings. So gimmel becomes a link or a joint, a connecting part. I like to think that the name still lives on in the north of England, where a passage connecting two roads or two blocks of houses is referred to as a ginnel, I believe."

Masters nodded. He had asked Benson to indulge his hobby, and the man was obeying. There were no grounds for complaint, but he wished they could get round to the business for which he had brought them here.

As if he could read the Superintendent's thoughts, Benson asked: "Have you ever heard of Nailsea glass?"

"I've heard of it. I know nothing about it."

"I'll show you some."

Benson got to his feet and limped across to a glass-fronted display cabinet. When he returned he was holding a small glass bell and a little model of a warship that reminded Masters very much of HMS *Victory*.

"Very nice indeed. Are these Nailsea glass?"

"Nailsea friggers."

"Friggers?"

"The glass workers used their spare time to make little things like this to give as gifts to their families and friends or for house decoration or simply for the amusement and satisfaction they derived from using their skill. Frigging—unlike its use today—meant producing ornamental and most unlikely objects like these in Nailsea glass. You'll have seen the famous yard-of-ale glasses?"

"Like a narrow trumpet with a ball at the bottom?" asked Green. "The ones you sometimes see in pubs?"

"Yes."

Masters handed the two pieces across to Green, and Benson sat down. "Nailsea was a place near Bristol where glass-making went on for about a hundred years from the late eighteenth to the late nineteenth century. From the factory there came glass walking sticks, pipes, trumpets, birds sitting on boughs and so on, including, I believe, the original glass rolling pins.

"These things became very popular, and so it became a commercial proposition to produce them for the market. Even after the Nailsea factory closed, other glass-makers went on producing the pieces which are still—erroneously—called Nailsea and regarded as antique in some quarters."

"But an expert could tell the difference?"

"Not all that easily. Modern pieces are still made of crude glass and to the original patterns, and that makes them hard to date unless they carry some symbol or motto—often of a romantic nature, because they were sometimes made as love tokens.

"But the point about Nailsea glass is that it often has spots in the glass, streaks, stripes or even coloured loops."

"Ah! And do I take it that no two pieces would, therefore, be exactly alike?"

"I think that is a safe assumption. The blemishes—or sometimes deliberate ornamentation—would identify a piece of Nailsea to those who were thoroughly familiar with it just as easily as a finger print would identify a man to an expert."

"Thank you, Mr Benson. That really was the chief fact I came to discover."

"But you went a roundabout way of asking."

"It is not always wise for people like us to be too direct. As you know, we've been in Limpid only a few hours. As far as we can tell, nobody in Limpid is above suspicion."

"Including me?" asked Benson, getting to his feet and holding out his hands for the tankards. "Refills? Or something different?"

"I'll stick to the same, please."

"And me," said Green.

As he went over to the wine cupboard, Masters nodded at Green who said: "In answer to your question, Mr Benson, the answer is yes."

"I thought it would be."

"Oh? Why?"

"Because not only am I related—no matter how tenuously—to this matter of gimmel flasks, but also because when I saw you this afternoon and realised who you were, I started to retrace my steps. Your arrival had interrupted what I was thinking about at the time and caused me to remember something I ought not to have forgotten, so I turned about immediately. You saw me do it. You were looking back through the car window. If I were a senior policeman and I saw that my appearance had caused somebody to change his plans, I would not only wonder why, I would wonder about the man himself. It must have seemed to be too much of a coincidence to disregard when you found that I was the man to whom Mrs Hardy had recommended you should come for information."

"You'd make a good policeman, sir," said Green as Benson handed him his beer.

"I have been something of a policeman in my time. Oh, not called one, of course, but in the old days we administered and policed our districts and areas. We had cases to dispose of from time to time."

"In that case," said Masters, "would you care to tell us what it was that our arrival caused you to remember? The thought that caused you to about-turn?"

"I shall comply with your wishes because I don't wish to be considered as hindering you, but it is the merest domestic detail."

"Nevertheless. . . ."

"Very well. I was wandering aimlessly when you stopped me. You see, I am a creature of habit and I was out of my stride. The first Tuesday in every month is auction day in Limpid, and I religiously set that day aside to be spent largely in the Corn Exchange. Today's sale was cancelled, and so my arrangements were uspet and I was at a loose end."

"Hence the walk."

"Quite. Your arrival brought me to my senses and reminded me that another of my habits on auction days is to take home meringues for tea. I pass the dairy which makes them, on my way to the Corn Exchange. I order them as I go and collect them on my way home. But because I did not go to the Exchange today, I failed to order the meringues. Quite frankly, I order them as a little treat for Mrs Taylor, my housekeeper. She dotes on them. I knew she would not consider the cancellation of the auction a good reason for not buying our habitual meringues. So not wishing to disappoint her—once my memory had been jolted by your cutting in on my thoughts—I immediately turned back in the hope that I wouldn't be too late to get the meringues. They're rather special ones, you see, and there is usually a run on them."

"You were successful, I hope, sir."

"Bessie had very kindly held two back for me. But whilst I've been prattling, Mr Masters, my mind has stumbled on something which may be a little more pertinent to your enquiry than my meringues."

"What would that be, sir?"

"On the first Tuesday in April—at the auction—there was actually a gimmel flask for sale in a mixed lot of glass which was simply catalogued as so many pieces of glassware."

The two detectives mentally sat up and took notice.

"So many pieces? How many?" queried Green.

"I believe twenty-seven. Yes, I'm sure it was twenty-seven. My memory for catalogue items is usually good, though as you have heard, it tends to gather wool at other times."

"All of this Nailsea stuff?"

"None of it. Just twenty-seven pieces of odds and bobs collected from round a house—tooth mugs, kitchen glasses, a broken butter dish, two old Pyrex plates and so on. Nothing of any value. The gimmel flask was not one of those it was difficult to date. It was an Italian, raffia-corked model of the second half of the twentieth century, as sold to tourists in souvenir shops."

"You saw it, yourself?"

"I examined it on the morning of the sale," admitted Benson.

"And decided not to bid for it."

"I had never intended to bid for it. But I have a young friend—a young married woman, wife of the photographer who takes pictures of my collection for insurance purposes—who, since she first came here with her husband, has started to take a great interest in objets d'art. She hasn't the money to dabble in a big way, of course, and indeed she has only just started to collect. But she saw the gimmel flask on viewing day and thought she might like it. She mentioned it to me—she was on the lookout for me as I went past the shop to the Corn Exchange—and asked me if I thought it might prove to be something worth having, disguised among a load of junk. The beginner is always hoping for such finds but they rarely happen, particularly when the dealers' ring is about. But I promised her I would look at it and give her an opinion. I told her that, from a collector's point of view, the flask was valueless."

"So you advised her not to buy."

"Not so. I'm a great believer in the old saw that beauty is in the eye of the beholder. If, after having my opinion of its value, Jill Racine still wanted to go ahead and buy for some other reason, then that was her affair."

"Did she buy?"

"Ah! That I don't know."

"You weren't at the sale to see if she bought or not?"

"I was at the sale until two o'clock, but the glassware in question came up later in the afternoon. The flask was of such little moment that when I next saw Jill I never thought to ask her if she had bid for it or not, and she didn't tell me. It may be that subconsciously I knew she wouldn't once I had declared it valueless. Such is my vanity, gentlemen."

"Fair enough," said Green. "But if Mrs Racine didn't buy the flask, who did?"

"I've no idea. But the offices of Hardy, Williams and Lamont are on the Market Hill, and every lot is booked in the buyer's name. Find the lot number in the catalogue and compare it with the invoice book."

Masters got to his feet. "Thank you very much, Mr Benson. I'm afraid we've trespassed too long on your time. It's after half past ten."

"Nonsense. I've enjoyed having you. Stay on and have a hot drink. You won't get anything in the Swan and Cygnets at this hour, you know. Mrs Taylor, my housekeeper, makes a very good cheese scone. I usually have one or two about now. Why not join me?"

Again an eye signal between Masters and Green. Then Green said: "We'd like to stay, sir and not only for the drink and scones."

"More information?"

"Of a general sort. Arising out of something you said earlier."

"What was that?"

"You said that beginners like Mrs Racine rarely found a treasure among old junk, particularly when there is a ring operating."

Benson nodded.

"Does that mean a ring operates here?"

"I'm afraid it does."

"Afraid? Because you know it's illegal?"

"I know it is illegal and so must the auctioneers. But the police appear to be unaware of it."

"Why?" asked Masters. "Because nobody has told them, or because they do not put in an appearance at the sales?"

"I would imagine the former, because the auction is held on private premises and so, presumably, policemen only have the right to attend as potential buyers or onlookers, not in their official capacity. But if anybody should inform the police, it ought to be the auctioneers, in my view."

"And in mine."

Benson got to his feet. "Come through and we'll brew up."

When they met in the interview room set aside for Masters' use in the Limpid police station the next morning, Masters said to Frimley and Hoame: "There is something I want to talk about before we move out."

"Oh, yes?" asked Frimley.

"It may colour our attitudes here, and may be of some use to us, so don't get the impression I am mentioning it just for fun or to point out any shortcomings on the part of your local force."

"This sounds serious. Is it?"

"It is law-breaking, certainly. I'm referring to the presence of a ring of about a dozen antique dealers who operate here once a month at the auction sales. For all I know, they may operate elsewhere round here, but for the moment I am interested in Limpid only."

"Go on," said Frimley heavily.

"Don't take it to heart, chum," said Green. "Whenever there's a murder we have to turn over stones which look nice and clean on top, but you should see what creeps out from under sometimes. The Chief is not blaming you. He blames the auctioneers for letting it go on under their noses and, knowing it to be illegal, not reporting it."

"I see. How does it operate?"

"According to my information, it is the marked catalogue system that's worked. To prevent puffers," said Masters.

"Puffers?"

"People who bid at an auction to raise the prices."

"What happens?"

"The individual dealers buy catalogues and view the lots. They then mark their catalogues with the top price they are willing to pay for any article. When they meet at the sale they work their way through the catalogues and declare their interest in whatever lots they would like to acquire. If only one person is interested in any item, nobody worries, and the interested party is given a clear run, knowing that none of his colleagues will puff. But if two or more have their eye on a good piece, then they have to declare their top price. Let us say the item in question is an antique bookcase which dealer A knows he can sell for four hundred pounds. He will fix his maximum bid at a price that will give him a very good profit margin. Say he decides on a maximum bid of a hundred and fifty."

"As low as that?"

"I am assured that would be his ceiling. Anyhow, the question is academic. The others who are interested in it are asked whether they are willing to go above a hundred and fifty. If nobody is prepared to do so, dealer A is in at his price.

"With no other dealers against him, the likelihood is that he will get it knocked down to him for far less than his one-fifty, unless a knowledgeable private collector is present and interested. The chances are that no ordinary lay people will force the bidding up to more than fifty or sixty. So dealer A buys his writing table for sixty pounds, and he then pays the ring the difference between what he actually paid and what he was prepared to pay to avoid being puffed. So he owes the ring ninety quid."

"I don't get it," said Reed. "What do they do with his ninety?"

"This will show you," said Masters, taking a sheet of paper and a pencil and talking as he wrote. "We'll use a simple ring of three dealers, A, B and C and give them just two bids each—bids which have topped those of their colleagues, and so are in without fear of puffing."

Masters showed them his table.

Dealer	Bid	Top Price (£)		Price Bid (£)		Into Ring (£)
A	1	150	—	60	=	90
B	1	30	—	10	=	20
C	1	70	—	30	=	40
A	2	100	—	50	=	50
B	2	40	—	30	=	10
C	2	60	—	30	=	30
						£240

A gets £250
worth of goods for £110 and has 50 × £5 units credit
B gets £70
worth of goods for £ 40 and has 14 × £5 units credit
C gets £130
worth of goods for £ 60 and has $\dfrac{26 \times £5}{90}$ units credit
units credit

"Notice they get a credit unit for every five pounds they are prepared to pay initially.

"The kitty collects £240 for 90 units of credit. Therefore one unit is worth two pounds sixty-seven. So dealer A draws out of the kitty £133, B draws £38 and C draws £69. So, what has happened? Look at the table, and you will see A has got £250 worth of goods for £110, and though he paid £140 in to the ring, he got £133 back, which means he paid seven pounds for the privilege of saving £140. B got £70 worth of goods for £40 and actually gets an eight pound bonus from the credits for not puffing his pals. C got £130 worth for £60 and pays one pound for the privilege of saving £70. Thus everybody in the ring wins, even on their own low valuations. The people who lose are the vendors who, being illegally robbed of the normal bidding system, are entirely at the mercy of the ring unless the articles have reserve prices put on them. If this happens, they are very likely not sold at all."

"And this is going on in Limpid?" asked Frimley.

"On the first Tuesday of every month among a dozen or so dealers making dozens of bids. The money involved is great."

"I don't believe it. No auctioneer would allow a ring to operate. He gets paid a percentage of takings. Low prices mean small percentages."

"Quite right," agreed Masters, "unless the ring is willing to reimburse the auctioneer for turning a blind eye to its activities. He takes fifteen per cent off the vendors. Why not fifteen per cent of the ring kitty? Say a kitty of four thousand pounds. That would give him a rake-off of six hundred a month, or seven thousand two hundred a year, tax free. How much do you have to earn to get that much, Wally?"

"God knows. At least fourteen or fifteen thousand, I suppose."

"Does it start to explain to you why rings are illegal and why Hardy—and presumably Williams and Lamont—are comparatively wealthy men all of a sudden?"

Frimley struck the desk with his fist. "I'll nail the bastards! Every single one of them. I'll have to bring in the Fraud Squad very likely to do the sums, but I'll get them."

"Hold it chum," said Green, lighting a crumpled Kensitas. "You haven't heard the best of it yet."

"No?"

"Lord save us," said Hoame. "And old Telford thought we could match your lot. In less than half a day!"

"Forget that," ordered Masters. "Listen to what we have to tell you and then put it right when the time comes. Hardy lived in Pellucid House, as you know. What did you think of it?"

"An enormous palace for two people," grated Frimley.

"And the contents? Didn't you recognise that all the pieces in that house were valuable? No? Well, I'll tell you, there was more there than any collector could hope to amass in a lifetime or many lifetimes."

"I don't know anything about antiques," snarled Frimley. It was very obvious that the crime squad man was getting angry both at the failure of the local police to stop this law-breaking on their patch, and at Masters' tone.

"Neither do I. But I ask, read, enquire."

"Okay. So you're Mr Know-all. Hardy had antiques which he obviously fiddled."

"Obviously. And I can give you a good idea of how it was done—if you're interested."

"I've got to be, haven't I?"

Masters looked at Green. "You tell them, Greeny."

Green, always ready to air his knowledge, took over willingly. "You've heard the Chief make an estimation of six hundred pounds a month going to the auctioneers from the ring. That isn't just guesswork, it is an estimation based on calculations made by a source we think we can trust."

"Only think?" asked Hoame.

"We asked the Yard to run a check on our informant late last night. We wanted a reply by breakfast time this morning, so the check was not as full and leisurely as it might otherwise have been. But as the person concerned was formerly a senior government official, Whitehall could supply at least a reasonable answer."

"Which was?"

"That the man was and is considered highly trustworthy and respected. He has, in his time, conducted a number of delicate missions of a secret nature for the government and on every occasion proved himself able and trustworthy. In addition—though this may not signify much—he was awarded a medal for gallantry in peace time."

"So?"

"So for the moment we trust him, particularly as he has expert knowledge of antiques and, again according to our report on him, contributes a learned column to one of the better known antique journals under the pseudonym of 'The Collector'. Those are our reasons for relying on what he has told us."

"And what's that? Apart from what we've already heard?"

"As I was saying, six hundred pounds goes each month from the ring to the auctioneers. There are three of them. Hardy is the senior partner. Here we are not on such firm ground, but we believe the money would have to be split among all three, but our guess is that it isn't split into three equal parts. One of the reasons for suggesting this is, for instance, that Lamont is far from flush with money, which he should be if he got a tax-free two hundred a month.

"We reckon that Hardy took three hundred, Williams and Lamont the rest, split either fifty-fifty or two-and-one. Whichever it is doesn't matter. The chances are that Hardy has been defrauding his own partners even further."

"How?"

"In getting the ring to act for him at the sales in return for turning a blind eye to their activities. Any piece he wants for himself out of the hundreds that pass through his hands on the way to the auctions he earmarks and asks the ring to bid for on his behalf."

"How is that defrauding his partners?"

"Let us use the same old antique bookcase which is worth four hundred nicker in a shop. Hardy asks the ring to bid and, as we have seen, the ring gets it for sixty. But at the end of the sale the ring owes Hardy his percentage of six hundred. So they knock sixty off six hundred and pay him five-forty. He goes along to Williams and Lamont and says: 'Sorry chums, only five-forty this month. That's two-seventy for me, one-eighty for Williams and ninety for Lamont.' So while his colleagues draw less because of his buy—which they know nothing about—Hardy gets cash and goods worth six hundred and seventy quid, with nobody any the wiser—least of all the tax man. What d'you reckon to that for a racket, Wally, my boy?"

Frimley was beyond words. He sat with both hands clenched just above the table. There was a pause while the others watched his mental struggle for expressions which would adequately describe his feelings of anger, dismay and—Masters guessed—an intense loss of pride caused by the fact that strangers could come into the area and unearth an adder's nest of crime in so short a time.

At last, Green said: "Forget it, chum. Nobody can prevent fraud. It's the cleaning up after that counts."

Hoame, who was as visibly uncomfortable as his Chief, asked: "Shall we tell Chief Superintendent Telford about this, Wally?"

"May I offer a word of advice?" asked Masters.

"Why not? You've been talking like a Dutch uncle all morning."

"Why not keep this under your hat until the murder case has been solved? By then, you should have enough solid information about the frauds to be able to satisfy Telford that you can come down hard on those involved with every chance of success. That will make him so happy he'll overlook the fact that the racket has been going on for some time."

"Present both cases at the same time as a sort of package deal, you mean?"

"That's right. So he has to accept it all or reject it all. And he won't be able to reject it if we arrest the murderer."

"Talking of that. . . ."

"Yes?"

"What's the form?"

"Well now, can we have some coffee brought in? Then we'll discuss our moves."

Hoame got on to the phone and ordered the refreshment.

"A lot of what I've said this morning may be relevant to the murder."

"You've certainly turned up enough material for a score of motives."

"Quite. But now we must get down to the mechanics of the thing. First of all I want to concentrate on the twin flask. I am told that one was in the auction a month ago. I want Greeny, Hoame and Berger to trace where it went and find if it is still about." Masters looked across at Green. "Carte blanche, Greeny. Play it as it comes."

"What about us?" asked Frimley.

"I want us to try and find out whether there are any other flasks about."

"Which could have been substituted for Hardy's? How do we go about it?"

"We find out who Hardy's friends were."

"Friends? I'd call anybody who slipped him a dose of croton oil an enemy."

"You're right. But whoever did it had to make two trips into Pellucid House. The way in may be covered by bushes and the summerhouse. . . ."

"You looked last night?"

"Yes. It seemed a reasonable thing to do in the cool of the evening. But as I was saying, whoever did that—four trips across that very large garden—could not guarantee that he would not be seen—from an upper window perhaps. Now for somebody who could not claim a good reason to be there, I consider that too big a risk to take. Don't forget that two of the journeys would have to be made after whoever did it had murdered Hardy. Now I know all about murderers returning to the scene of their crime. But not like this. So I would suggest that whoever made those journeys was so well known and friendly with the

Hardys that he could claim he was on a drop-in social visit."

"Not if he was seen sulking in the bushes, he couldn't."

"Oh yes he could," countered Green. "In fact it would suit him down to the socks. He could say he had seen a suspicious figure lurking there and he'd left the path to find out what this character was up to. A lovely excuse. It immediately makes everybody believe there was a stranger about."

Hoame sighed and then called exasperatedly: "Come in," as he heard a tap at the door. He carried on with what he was about to say while the coffee was being put on the table. The gist of what he said was that the Yard men could make black look like white, turn disadvantage into advantage, find reasonable causes for patently unreasonable actions and because of this ability, he surmised that they, too, must be near-crooks and beyond the understanding of poor rural dicks and jacks such as saw to the keeping of the law in Limpid and its environs.

"Sugar?" asked Masters when Hoame had finished, and pushed the bowl across to him.

"Don't get an inferiority complex, son," advised Green. "George here is a smart-Alec. And some of it's rubbed off on us. Reed and Berger aren't too contaminated yet, but they're sitting there drinking it in at a merry rate." Green took a slurp of his coffee, grimaced at the taste and went on: "If you're tough enough to drink this very often, nothing we say or do should upset you."

Hoame had the grace to grin.

"It is pretty bloody foul, isn't it?"

Masters nodded assent and then said: "Colin, the flask you're after is important."

"Why?"

"It might have occurred to you to wonder why the murderer didn't replace Hardy's flask when he removed the one with poison in it. It could be because he had to use Hardy's stoppers in the poison bottle, because the one sold here had raffia stoppers."

"Why not switch the stoppers back again?"

"Because they were contaminated. He didn't want to kill again."

"Sensitive, was he?"

"If you like. But the fact remains that he didn't replace Hardy's bottle and it could have been because the substitute had different stoppers—and that could mean it was the raffia-topped one sold locally. So I want to know where it went."

The meeting began to break up a minute or two later. As he and Masters walked out to the cars together—out of earshot of the remainder, Green said: "That bit about the stoppers that you fed to Colin."

"What about it?"

"It sounded fine. I know these locals want to have a material reason for anything they do, so you gave Colin Hoame a tangible fact he could appreciate."

"Just to spur him on."

"I know. But he's with me, don't forget. I don't want to be fed a load of old bull."

"True. Can't you disregard the bit about the stoppers being contaminated and the murderer being so sensitive as not to wish to kill a second time?"

"I can. I have done. But you mentioned it to Hoame to drive home the fact that the flask at the auction is important, and I can't see why. Suppose we found some old biddy bought it and still has it?"

"It will still be important."

"Why, for god's sake."

Masters leaned against the car. "We have a clever murderer with a lot of courage."

"Right."

"He had to get to the house to remove the flask. Why?"

"It might have incriminated him."

"True. But replacing the original harmless flask would have put the local police off the scent altogether. That would have lessened the chances of his incriminating himself even further. So why not do it?"

"He forgot?"

"We'd decided he was clever."

"So what?"

"Don't you think then that we should look for a clever reason for not returning the original flask, rather than just assuming that the murderer was forgetful?"

"You've got a point. Any guesses as to what the clever reason could be?"

"I think so. How about his intention of making us concentrate on the gimmel flask?"

"If that was it, he's succeeding. You are concentrating on it just as he wanted you to."

"But with my eyes open."

"Why do as he wants—even with your eyes open?"

"Because I want to know why he wanted us to concentrate on it. And when we learn that we should be a little nearer the answer to the whole affair?"

Green sucked a tooth.

"A pity you didn't give that load in there this explanation. That would really have made them wonder what they've struck."

Masters grinned.

"I like to keep something in the family, Greeny."

CHAPTER V

The offices of Hardy, Williams and Lamont were pretty foul, too. As Hoame led him in, Green glanced around. "I thought this sort of sludge brown varnish paint went out with Queen Victoria."

"Nobody could accuse this lot of being the hard and bright type of modern estate agent."

"Lack of competition?" suggested Berger.

"Maybe. They're the biggest crowd around here."

"The board in the window with the property for sale looked freshly done. It doesn't look as though they have much difficulty in getting rid of places."

"So they don't have to paint up," said Green, glancing with distaste at the worn, brown, oak-block lino in the narrow hall. "This hasn't even seen a duster since the year spit."

Hoame grinned. "I reckon you boys could draw an inference even from that."

"Of course," said Green airily. "In the lean years when they weren't making money they couldn't afford cleaners. Then they started to coin it, but they could see no reason why they should start handing it out again when they'd got by previously." He turned to

Hoame and said, surprisingly, "The child is father to the man, laddie."

Their voices must have been overheard, because the door on the right of the hall, leading to the front room in whose window the notices were displayed, opened and a bespectacled man appeared. He was wearing a not-quite-navy-blue suit with a heavy chalk stripe. His voice was not displeasing as he asked: "Can I help you, gentlemen?"

"Police," said Hoame.

"Oh! Who do you wish to see?"

"You're the chief clerk, aren't you?"

"Yes."

"Then you'll do. This your office?"

Green said more courteously than Hoame, "We have a question you might help us with, Mr . . . er. . . ."

"Fletcher. It's on the door."

"So it is. Mr Bernard Fletcher. So, sir, may we come in?"

Fletcher withdrew into the room and they followed him.

"What is it you want to know?"

"An extract from your records, please."

"Records? Our business affairs are private."

"Sit down, laddie," said Green kindly, "and just understand that nothing is private in a murder investigation. Once you've appreciated that, you'll recognise the value of unstinting co-operation. Now . . . god! this office is filthy. Would you mind dusting the corner of that desk so's I can sit down? Those pigeon-holes? What are they for? The rubbish in there hasn't been cleared out for years. Now, where was I? Ah, yes. Records. Show me your sale catalogue for

last month and your invoice book with the auctioneer's slips."

"They're all correct and they balance. Everything
has been paid for. We run a cash business."

"Even with dealers?"

"Which dealers?"

"Come on, son, don't try to stall. Where are the
documents?"

"In the general office. It's at the back. I'll get
them."

"Stay where you are, Mr Fletcher. Berger, slip into
the general office and ask the head typist for the
books I want, will you."

Berger left and Green said to Hoame: "We'd better
have the catalogues for the last six or eight months,
too."

"There aren't any spares," said Fletcher. "Only the
file copies."

"Don't talk rubbish, lad. You've got a photocopier
in that general office of yours, haven't you? How else
do you circulate details of properties? I'm not going
to believe you still cyclostyle them. You would if you
could, of course, to save expense, but I bet you can't
find girl typists these days willing to get their fingers
inky on one of those old machines."

"I think I had better call Mr Williams or Mr Lamont."

"Go ahead, lad. I shall want to see them, and it
might as well be sooner as later."

It was the old ploy, and it took the wind out of
Fletcher's sails. He was sitting back on the round-
backed horsehair chair that did him for a desk chair.
It was fairly obvious that Hardy, Williams and La-

mont, being in the second-hand business, were not god's gift to office equipment salesmen.

Berger came back with the required documents. Green, who knew the lot he was looking for was in the second half of the catalogue, instructed Berger to get copies of catalogues for the whole of the last year.

Green laid the catalogue aside and picked up the invoice book. He turned the leaves, checked with the catalogue again, then looked up.

"Don't keep very good records, do you?"

"We do."

"Then perhaps you will tell me why lot 139 is only marked down to 'B' and not to an identifiable buyer."

Hoame began to whistle quietly to himself, as though bemused. He had known this Yard crowd less than twenty-four hours, but he would have been willing to bet that there would be something wrong with the record of sale of any lot they had decided to check. It was—to him—uncanny. He had not yet appreciated how much hard work and thought there was behind the overt moves they made.

"That 'B' stands for Bert. He's our head porter. We don't write it out in full for Bert. He often does a bit of buying for people who can't get to the sales. Nothing big. Just small things."

"Small things are sometimes very valuable."

"Not this sort of small thing. It was a job lot of glassware."

"I see. Now, can you tell me. . . ."

The door opened and a man walked in. He was, Green guessed, in his middle thirties and was running to fat. The hair, which was thinning noticeably on top, was nevertheless long at the sides and back.

Unattractively so, because it had none of the crispness and life that hair, if it is to be worn long, must have. In this case the man merely looked as if he was long overdue for a haircut and shampoo, and the shoulders of his grey jacket carried a goodly sprinkling of dandruff.

"What's going on here?" The tone was intended to be authoritarian, but in spite of the spirit willing it, the flesh—in the form of the voice—was not quite up to it. The tone was a petulant squawk. "What's this circus going on in here, Fletcher?"

Green didn't like it. "Circus?" he asked quietly.

A more sensitive man would have scented danger. But the newcomer ploughed on. "This is a business house. Who are these people, Fletcher? Get rid of them. I can hardly hear myself think in my office."

"Sorry, Mr Lamont, but these are policemen."

Green slid off the desk and planted himself in front of the junior partner. "So you're Lamont, are you?"

"Mr Lamont to you."

"You'll be lucky if you're not known by a number before you're much older."

"Don't be ridiculous. What could you charge me with?"

"Well, to start with, in the last two minutes you have urged your chief clerk to get rid of me. It is an offence to incite others to commit an offence, and if Fletcher tried to get rid of me it would constitute a flagrant case of attempting to impede an officer in carrying out his duty. I could wheel you off to the nick for that right now."

"I didn't know you were policemen."

"Where the hell do you think the saying that ignorance of the law is no excuse came from? And for god's sake stop sweating lad. It'll begin to stink like a rugby fifteen's dressing room in here soon."

"What do you want to know?"

"From you? At the moment? Nothing, lad. We're dealing with Mr Fletcher. Until you urged him not to be he was being very co-operative. Now, unless you have some urgent business in here, how about letting us get on and we'll away inside ten minutes."

Green closed the door after the departing Lamont. As he turned to speak to Fletcher he saw Hoame and Berger holding a whispered conversation near the window. He moved across and heard Hoame say: "Do it discreetly. I want them all for the past twelve months."

"What?" whispered Green.

"Their invoice books. It occurred to me that if we want to make the fraud charges stick we ought to nab the evidence before it's destroyed."

"Clever thinking, laddo. You're learning fast."

Green returned to Fletcher.

"'B' for Bert. Bert who? And where is he?"

"Bert Horner. He'll be in the repository. We couldn't hold yesterday's sale, so the stuff's had to go back inside, and there's next month's stuff starting to come in. It's a hell of a mess because the stuff already in there will be wanted first."

"Hard cheddar, chum. Where's this repository?"

"I know where it is," said Hoame. "It's the old flour mill, isn't it?"

"Is it on the phone?" asked Green.

"Sorry," said Fletcher, "no. What would be the point?"

"I see what you mean." Green took out a pristine

packet of Kensitas and handed them round. "I reckon we've just time to smoke these before we push off."

Hoame, realising Green was playing for time to let Berger collect the invoice books, agreed. Before the fags were finished the D.C. was back with a couple of large, bulging envelopes. Nobody could tell what the contents were without looking inside. Certainly Fletcher didn't seem to have a clue.

As Masters and Frimley climbed into the car, Reed asked: "Where to, sir?"

"The corner of the High Street. I want to call on a Mr Richard Benson."

"The antiques buff! Is he the one you saw last night?" asked Frimley.

"Yes. Do you know him?"

"I've seen him about. He looks a cut above most people. Quite a gent, I believe."

"If by that you mean that your observations and local opinion seem to corroborate the official report on him, I'm happy to hear it. I like sound sources."

It took the car about two minutes to reach its destination. They crossed the road and rang Benson's bell. Again the wait before Benson appeared.

"Good morning, Superintendent. I hadn't expected to see you again so soon. Sorry for the wait, but had you called at this time on any other day except Wednesday, Mrs Taylor would have been here to let you in, and she's much quicker on the stairs than I am."

"I'm sorry to trouble you again so soon, Mr Benson."

"No trouble, I assure you. Come along up. The percolator is on."

"We'd rather not, sir, if you don't mind, because we're in working hours, now. Oh, by the way, let me introduce Superintendent Frimley of your local crime squad and Detective Sergeant Reed of my team."

"How d'you do, both of you. Now, Masters, what can I do for you?"

"I want you to tell me, if you can, whether there are any gimmel flasks in the area other than the two we talked of last night."

"The answer to that is that I am morally certain there must be a few more. They are by no means rare. But I can give you no clue as to their whereabouts. They could literally be anywhere."

"I understand that, sir. But collectors tend to specialise in certain areas of the antique spectrum, don't they? Who, of your knowledge, is a collector—in a professional or amateur way—who might be interested in Nailsea glass and might, therefore, conceivably have acquired a gimmel flask?"

"Collectors are rather more rare than the flasks," said Benson. "I can suggest nobody except Mrs Horbium, who is rather catholic in her tastes and tends to amass anything and everything she thinks may be vaguely antique. Not furniture. Smaller items."

"Nobody else?"

"Nobody. But I'm sure the dealers might muster a few."

"Dealers in Limpid?"

"There is only one. You'll see it on the Market Hill. A furnisher's. Next door to a television rental shop. But away from Limpid, practically every village has its antique shop."

"I see. Now, could you give me Mrs Horbium's address?"

"She lives in Dew-pond Cottage, which is one of a row opposite the playing field on the London Road. Some way past where you met me yesterday. You met Mrs Wellerby, last night. She has taken the cottage next door, called Ox-bow Cottage. It belongs to Mrs Horbium who, I think, owns the whole row. They're very attractive and occupied by elderly colonels and their ladies. A very select row of cottages indeed."

The cottages were certainly attractive, if not of proven selectivity. The row was end-on to the main road, but set far enough back for the nearest one to be well clear of pounding traffic. Originally a narrow walk had passed the front doors and separated the front gardens from the cottages. Now the front garden fences had disappeared. The walk had been widened and paved, the gardens had been gravelled. So the cottages could be easily reached on foot, and the gravelled area catered for cars. Surrounding the gravel were well-tended flower beds. The back gardens each had a garage set at an angle of forty-five degrees to the main road and the tarmac roadway which had been put down to serve them. By this echelon plan, it had been possible to make the little service road quite narrow, since no room was needed for a vehicle to turn at right angles. The whole row was decorated white, with front doors in a variety of colours carried out in the highest gloss paint. Masters could appreciate why Benson had spoken of the row as he did. There was an air of quiet affluence and screaming cleanliness about the place.

Ox-bow Cottage took no finding. The expert tinkling of a piano sounded through an open window.

"Joanna Wellerby practising," said Masters as the

noise of the engine died and the brush of the tyres on gravel allowed the notes to come clearly. "It's an ability I wish I had."

"You, Chief?" asked Reed. "A pianist?"

"Why not?"

"Because you're a man with . . . well, sir, you're too direct, too manly . . . you haven't got that sort of temperament."

"I don't know whether that's a compliment or not, Sergeant. But the fact remains that if I could run up and down scales like that I'd be a very contented man."

Frimley said: "The other man's grass is always greener. You're a contented man now, because you're as much a professional at your job as she is at hers. More so, probably. She's only on the upper branches, not the very top one. You are. I read that article by that German detective. I can remember what he said. 'Masters is the man on whom all police detectives the world over should model themselves, even if few will ever emulate him.' "

"That bloke was talking through the top of his Germanic cap. I'd entertained him to a good dinner the night before he wrote that."

They left the car. The scales had given way to Beethoven. They passed the open window and found Dew-pond Cottage. The door was painted *eau de nil.*

Mrs Horbium was at home. Today she was in a frock of what looked like silk material. At any rate, to Masters' untutored eye, it shone like silk. It was basically old gold or copper colour, with a pattern of rectangles in blue and red, like patches of four by two set higgledy-piggledy all over it, each surrounded by a frame of white a quarter of an inch wide. It had

short sleeves, considerably wider than Mrs Horbium's
very fat arms which, though smooth and white inside,
seemed to be dotted with innumerable reddish
pimples on the backs of the upper parts. The dress
was cut too low in a bound V in front. Mrs Horbium's cleavage was too big for the escapement. From
Masters' height it was like looking down into some
crevasse from which those unlucky enough to fall in
would never emerge. On her blue hair—not covering
it, but planted cornerwise across it like some mortar
board that had lost its cap-piece—was a brightly
coloured head-scarf, held on by heaven knew what
sort of mechanism. On her hands she had canary-
coloured rubber gloves, and on her feet a pair of
oldish white sandals now relegated to working shoes.

"Mr Masters." She was coy. "And friends, I see.
Come to call on me. But I thought your Mr Green
said you wouldn't be interviewing everybody in Limpid."

"Good morning, Mrs Horbium. May I present my
colleagues: Detective Superintendent Frimley, whom
you may know by sight as he is local, and another
member of my team, Detective Sergeant Reed. We are
still not proposing to interview everybody in Limpid,
but we have come to you specially because we think
you may be able to help us and to give us some advice."

"Oh, do come in. Come in. And excuse me a moment while I tidy myself. Housework, you know, has
to be done."

"Thank you. But please don't put yourself out on
our account. I assure you it isn't necessary and you
look very nice in your working clothes. The headscarf
is particularly fetching."

"Do you think so?" She wobbled down the tiny hall in front of them, the sea-roll induced by her enormous waves of flesh carrying her at every step to within an inch of one wall or the other of the passage. "This is my sitting room. There are enough chairs for everybody."

It was garish. But Masters realised, with something of a shock, that had it not been so, he would have been disappointed. The right decor for any room, he supposed, was the one which matched the personality of the owner. He would expect Mrs Horbium to overwhelm in some way. Here she had overwhelmed with colour, amount of furnishing, mixture . . . in fact, in every way possible, with no regard for period, style or motif.

Over the modern fireplace was a Victorian overmantle with a square mirror in the middle and a host of little shelves and brackets, each one crammed with bric-à-brac, some of it attractive—in Masters' eyes—much of it so appalling he would never have afforded it house room. The picture rail was still there, and along its length, cheek by jowl, were decorative plates. Elsewhere on the walls were fretwork brackets such as were done fifty years ago by youths in woodwork classes, much as their sisters wove samplers for needlework. Each bracket was laden with as many articles as it could carry.

But the chairs were comfortable and accepted them well enough. Their hostess left them temporarily with a squawked desire to be excused, and in no time at all was back with a collapsible three tier cake stand in one hand and a large, round brass tray in the other. On her second journey she brought in the folding legs to convert the tray to a table. Before Masters could protest she had gone again, and next time came back with a cream-filled sponge cake, a plate of individual cream cakes and a plate of biscuits. As she put them on the cake stand she explained that she always had a little snack in the middle of the morning as she didn't usually eat much breakfast.

Then the coffee and cups came in and she sat down to preside. She would accept no refusal, and in the face of such kindness it was difficult to be adamant. Besides, thought Masters, the more of her cream cake they ate, the bigger the favour they would be doing her, for he was now pretty sure that her size was not due to some physical defect but simply to a voracious appetite.

"This is nice," she said, biting into a squidgy wedge of cake. Masters wasn't sure whether she was referring to their visit or the food, but he replied courteously: "Very nice, indeed."

"How?" she asked, using her tongue to take a stray blob of cream from the corner of her mouth, "How can I help you?"

"I wondered whether you happened to have in your collection a gimmel flask."

"There now!" She put down her plate. "Isn't it always the same! You never hear a word for years and then if you do suddenly hear it, you hear it twice ever so quickly."

"Which word, Mrs Horbium? Gimmel?"

"Yes. I didn't even know it myself until Mr Lamont used it a week or two ago, and now you use it."

"But you know what I mean by gimmel flasks?"

"Yes. What I used to call twin bottles."

"Mr Lamont told you what they were, I suppose?"

"Oh, no! I don't like to show my ignorance. I

looked it up later. I was quite surprised to see what it meant."

"I see. Have you got one?"

"Oh, yes I have, somewhere."

"Would you mind checking for me?"

"Not in the least. It is in the dining room. In the sideboard."

"You use it for salad oil and vinegar?"

"Oh, no. I like my mayonnaise."

"I'll bet she does," said Reed when their hostess had left them. "Anything fattening and she's after it like a long dog. Cream cakes for mid-mornings!"

"Here you are. Just where I thought it was. It's a bit dusty, I'm afraid, because I haven't cleaned those cupboards out for ages. There is so much to dust in this house."

They all silently agreed with her as she handed the flask to Masters.

"Why are you interested in gimmel flasks? Are you a collector, too?" Before Masters could reply, she went on, "I'm not a real collector. Or should I say I collect quite a lot, as you can see." She waved an arm like a leg of mutton round the room. "And there's more, everywhere in the house. But it's a mania with me. Like eating." She giggled. "Everybody is always telling me I eat too much and collect too much. One gentleman was quite rude about it. He said that over-collecting should be called a sickness—of mind and body—and that I also made over-eating a sickness. But for me, a large number of just one type of antique is not as interesting as an assortment—a sort of general collection which I can't fit into my home. I've been quite successful at fitting it all in, don't you think?"

"Yes, ma'am," said Reed, with an amount of feeling which left Masters wondering whether the sergeant had misunderstood Mrs Horbium's drift and had thought she was referring to the actual housing of her collection rather than to the dimension it added to her home.

"I don't make a serious study you see. I just pick and choose. At the moment I'm having quite a flirtation with pot lids."

"With what?" asked Frimley in amazement.

"Pot lids. I will show you some." She crossed to one of the brackets and came back with three circular ceramic lids. "There you are. One from a bear's grease jar, one from tooth paste and one from cold cream. Cherry tooth paste and Rose cold cream! Charming. And don't forget potted shrimps. These lids, you know, really served as the labels for the jars. Early advertising, in fact. As you can see, most lids were black and white, but some are coloured. I haven't any coloured ones yet. But don't you think that dancing bear is sweet? One of these days I shall go on a dig."

"Dig? What for?" asked Frimley.

"Pot lids, of course. The best place to find them is on a pre-1895 rubbish dump. They were thrown away as rubbish then, and because most rubbish in those days was used for land reclamation you can find them by digging at the mouth of the Thames or at filled-in clay pits. And alongside canal banks. A lot of local authorities, in whose areas canals were being dug, seized the opportunity to bury their rubbish under the excavated soil thrown up to form the banks and tow paths. Joanna and I are thinking of trying our hand this summer."

"Your daughter, Joanna?" asked Frimley.

"Oh dear, no. Joanna Wellerby, the pianist. She's taken the cottage next door. Very suitable for her, because there is one big room through from front to back, big enough to take her piano very comfortably and to make quite a studio for her. Her husband left her, you know, and as she was born near Limpid she came back here when her marriage broke down. I knew her mother, and I was able to help her, because these cottages are all mine, and I had one empty. I had thought of setting out my collection in there, but Joanna's need was greater than mine."

"Is she interested in antiques?" asked Masters.

"Oh, no. Her aesthetic cravings are amply satisfied by her music, though she is becoming a little interested since she got to know Mr Lamont. I told you he mentioned a gimmel flask to her a few weeks ago and, of course, she sees my collection." She stopped suddenly and opened her eyes wide. "You never told me why you are interested in gimmel flasks. Do you want to buy one?"

Masters ignored the last part and simply asked: "Do you really not know why we are interested in gimmel flasks?"

"Why should I know?"

"Haven't you heard how Mr Hardy died?"

"Oh yes. Very sad. He was poisoned, or so Maud told me."

"Mrs Hardy didn't tell you what the poison was?"

"She didn't know. She said the police didn't know on Sunday and on Monday they refused to tell her."

"Right enough," said Frimley. "Nobody knew what the poison was until the pathologist found out.

Besides, we packed Mrs Hardy off to her room soon after we arrived on the scene."

"But Mrs Hardy did know how you thought the poison was administered."

"Oh yes," answered Frimley. "We had to question her as to what he had eaten. The table was still laid of course, and after she'd told us what he'd had and we couldn't find the oil and vinegar, she told us it was in a double bottle. As you know, it had gone, and its disappearance told us what we wanted to know. The pathologist simply told us what the poison was."

Mrs Horbium could hardly wait for Frimley to finish speaking. "You mean the poison was in their gimmel flask?"

"That's right. Didn't Mrs Hardy tell you?"

"I suppose she forgot," said Mrs Horbium, and then with an unusual sensitivity added, "and I could hardly ask her, could I?"

Masters smiled. "So now, Mrs Horbium, you see why we are interested in the flasks." As he said it, he realised she couldn't possibly know his theory about a second flask having replaced the first, but nevertheless she said she understood.

As Masters got to his feet, he said: "Is Mrs Wellerby a great friend of Mr Lamont's from the old days? They're of an age, perhaps?"

"They're about the same age, certainly, but Joanna didn't know him until quite recently. Between you and me, Mr Masters, I think she sees too much of him. He is a married man, after all. But there, I suppose I'm old-fashioned. There are no rules of conduct these days, are there?"

*   *   *

Hoame directed Berger to drive down the London Road a short way and then to turn right. After less than a hundred yards they came to another major road parallel to the London Road. But Mill Road was the old packway and so was narrower and less able to take the traffic that used it. Along Mill Road were some of Limpid's oldest buildings, and these were suffering sadly, flaking and crumbling under the constant earth tremors caused by the haulage vehicles. Berger drove slowly, taking a gently weaving course, past old shops and, in places, lath and daub buildings. Then the road began to dip down the side of the low hill on which Limpid had originally been built. At one point, the road and the river came together, and though Mill Road turned away again, here had been the old ford over the Clear, the river which, with the hill, had determined the original site of Limpid. Slightly upstream of the ford was the mill itself, a broad-based, stunted tower of wood, the horizontal slats of which had once gleamed white, but which under the aegis of Hardy, Williams and Lamont had turned to the grey of bare weathered timber.

The car left the road and hairpinned back on the little track down to the mill. The double front doors of the ground floor were wide open. Berger pulled up in front of them.

"Hoy!" yelled a voice from inside. "You can't park there. We wanna get out."

As Green disembarked he said, "Drive on a few yards, son," and then, accompanied by Hoame, he entered the dim interior of the mill. All about him, piled between the pillars that supported the floor above, were heaps of furniture, some showing lot labels. Ahead of him was an old, shabby blue furniture van, and sitting on an old kitchen chair with his back to its bonnet was a man.

"Are you the one who shouted, mate?"

"Yes, I am. That's a private road to the mill. You've no business parking there."

"Ah, but I have."

Somewhere behind the van a rather tuneless voice broke into song. "Tina, soon the leaves will be falling, From the pine-lands I'm calling, Won't you come back to me-e?"

"Good lord," said Hoame. "What was that?"

"That's Bandy," said the man, and then added by way of explanation, "singing."

"Just the two of you here?" asked Green.

"Who wants to know?"

"Cut it out," growled Berger who had joined them. "This is Detective Chief Inspector Green."

"Police, are you? Well there's nothing here for you. The lorry's all right since we had the tail light done."

Green stared at him. He was paunchy and unshaven. He wore scuffed brown shoes which ought to have had laces and hadn't, and bulged in places as though the wearer were a chronic sufferer from corns and bunions. The dirty grey trousers had seen better days. He was wearing a green baize bib apron and over it an old grey jacket. He had a greasy tie on a woollen collar and on his head he wore a greasy old trilby.

"I asked if there were just the two of you here?"

"Only me an' Bandy 'cept on sale days, then we signs on old Jeff an' Gil Dunn, just to give a hand with the lifting like."

"Then you must be Bert Horner."

"That's right. Bert an' Bandy Horner, Removals."

"I thought you worked for Hardy, Williams and Lamont."

"We do, most of the time. But we're available for hire. It's our van, you see. Bandy's driver, I'm boss."

There was the noise of something heavy being dragged over the uneven, red brick floor of the mill.

"Bandy seems to do all the work, too."

"He's younger'n me."

"And thinner, too, I expect. Right, Bert. At the April sales in the Corn Exchange you bought lot number one three nine; twenty-seven pieces of assorted glassware."

"What if I did?"

"I want to know what you did with it."

"Nothing."

"You must have wanted it for something, or you wouldn't have bought it."

"An' that's where you're wrong. I didn't buy it for myself, see."

"Who for, then?"

"I was biddin' for Mr Lamont, as the auctioneers aren't allowed to when they're on the stand."

"For Lamont? What would he want a job lot of glassware for?"

"He didn't."

Green was beginning to lose his temper. "Now look, matey, don't try to be funny with me. You said Lamont asked you to bid for and buy a lot he didn't want."

"He thought he did when he told me. Then after the sale he came up to me, said he'd had a look at the stuff and it wasn't what he'd thought. He told me I could have it. Cost him 30p, it did, so he wasn't bust by that, was he?"

"What did you do with it?"

Bert lifted up his voice. "Bandy!"

" 'Ello!"

"Where's them old glasses and things from last sale that Lamont didn't want?"

Bandy came from wherever he'd been working and rounded the van to join the party.

"Why?"

"These gents want to look at 'em."

"To buy? Let 'em go for a quid."

"They're the police, Bandy."

"Oh!"

"Where are they?"

"Along here."

They were stacked on top of an old chest of drawers. Green looked at them and then counted. "There should be twenty-seven pieces. There's only twenty-six here. Where's the other one?"

"Other one? What other one?"

"There was a sort of bottle with two necks."

"That's right, Bert," said Bandy. "I remember, when we laid them out. Green thing with bits of red and yellow raffia on it."

"Well don't ask me. I never saw it. That's just as it was when I got it from the 'Change."

"Does anybody else ever come in here?"

"Fletcher comes in to make up lots sometimes. If it's a houseful, one of the partners goes with Fletcher to do it on site. But if odd bits come in here to be added on, Fletcher does it himself. And believe you me, mister, if Fletcher says there was twenty-seven bits of glass there, there was twenty-seven."

"Anybody else?"

"No. Only the two I told you about, and they don't come in here. They go to the 'Change to handle at the sale."

"So where did that bottle go missing?"

"In the 'Change after the sale. It's hell's delight in there then. People paying and claiming. Fletcher saying, 'Bert! Number forty-seven, six dining chairs for Mr Whatsisname here!' And I has to get them out where we've stacked 'em, an' they're allus at the bottom of the heap. Everybody's working, an' buyers are picking up their bits an' pieces off the tables—aye, an' leaving stuff."

"Leaving it, after they've paid for it?"

"When it's a composite lot, yeah. Say you've got a pressure cooker an' eight bowls in one lot, an' some woman bids 'cos she wants a pressure cooker but doesn't want a load of old cracked bowls, she takes the cooker an' leaves the bowls for us to clear up."

"Are you telling me," asked Green, "that you and Bandy boy here don't make a bob or two out of what's left? To second-hand dealers and such like?"

"Well, we 'as to dispose of it somehow. Dustmen won't take it."

"They do more than make a bob or two," said Hoame. "I've just remembered. I've heard of you two characters, but I'd forgotten the name."

"Oh, yes?"

"Timber. You collect all the old furniture and take it to bits and sell the wood."

"What about it?"

"I wonder how many wardrobes are broken accidentally-on-purpose so they can't go into the sale, but can be broken up for planks of oak and mahogany?"

"Wait a minnit, mister. . . ."

"It's all right, Bert. I'm not complaining. But don't try to tell the Chief Inspector you never get any perks. Especially after Bandy wanted to charge us a quid for that glassware you got for nothing."

"It's good wood. People making things like a bit of seasoned oak or bird's eye maple at half price."

"I'm sure. Do you plane it up for them?"

"That'd cost more."

"I bet it would. You're making a packet, Bert. And don't forget in future that I know all about it." Hoame sounded as if he'd come to the conclusion that all the citizens of Limpid were either corrupt or on the make-haste and he was going to keep an eye on things from now on.

Green looked at his watch. "Time we were getting back to the pub for lunch. Care to join us for a pint, Colin?"

"I might just do that." He turned to Bert. "Watch your step, you two."

When they were in the car, Berger said: "I thought they genuinely didn't know what had happened to that flask, sir."

"Bert didn't. He's too idle. But Bandy knows there's something on. He's fly. Senior coppers don't chase after useless bits of glassware in his opinion. He's mistaken, of course. I've chased after useless bits of paper and fag ends in my time. But Bandy won't realise that. He's thinking things over. Wondering if he saw anything significant at that sale, or else he's simply putting two together, and wondering what's in it for him."

"You reckon he's not above a bit of blackmail, sir?"

"Seeing the environment in which he works," said

Hoame bitterly, "would there be anything odd if he were a villain? If environment counts for anything he'll be up to all the crimes in the calendar."

"Take it easy," said Green. "Keep a sense of proportion, mate. You can't afford to get emotional about this. If you play it right, you're going to sort them all out."

"It's like ground elder," replied Hoame. "Once you get it you can't get rid of it."

"I can't say you're wrong, chum," replied Green, "because I reckon there's more to come."

CHAPTER VI

Masters and his two companions arrived at the Swan and Cygnets shortly after Green's party.

"Six minds with but a single thought."

"If they're all like mine, Mr Masters," said Hoame, "they're not focused on beer."

"Develop two planes of thought," said Masters. "It's important. School yourself and think of beer—or anything else for that matter—and meanwhile push the case into the back of your mind without dismissing it altogether. If you can achieve that, you'll never be caught out. People will call you jammy and say you can't even stop for a pint of beer without some clue dropping into your lap. They'll be wrong, of course, because while you're drinking you'll still be on the job, working twice as hard as they are and thoroughly earning or deserving your luck."

"Is that what you do?"

"I try to. For instance, I've noticed that while I've been talking to you, Mr Richard Benson, who is not unconnected with this case, has come into the bar."

"So?"

"So I ask myself why he has come. Has he just

dropped in for a drink, or has he come in in the hope of seeing somebody?"

"You, for instance?"

"Perhaps."

"You can't say he has."

"Of course I can't, but it's a possibility I must consider. If I am pretty sure he would like to say something to me but isn't quite sure how to approach me, I must make the effort to give him his chance."

"For all you know he could hate the sight of you."

"I know he doesn't."

"How?"

"Because he knows I am staying at this pub and that I'm not a teetotaller. It is, therefore, on the cards that should he come in here he would see me."

"He couldn't be a hundred per cent certain."

"Of course not. But it is a risk—if he were trying to avoid me."

"It could be that he doesn't care either way."

"That, too. But I know that he doesn't frequent this or any other pub at nights because I found him at home last night. Furthermore he keeps a very well-stocked drinks cupboard which includes beer. This leads me to believe he is a home drinker. I can't think that he keeps such a stock for visitors. Nor do I believe he is a heavy enough drinker to drink at home and at a pub."

"You've now talked me into believing that he cannot have come here for any purpose except to see you."

"That was my intention."

"But he has made no move to contact you."

"Because he is a man of innate courtesy and would

not intrude while I was in conversation with a colleague on what might well be professional business."

Hoame put his empty glass down. "Mr Telford knew what he was doing when he accepted, on our behalf, a few days tuition from you in direction. Have another, sir."

"No, thank you. I have to see a man about an antique."

But Masters was wrong. It was not an antique. It was a property deal.

"Mr Masters," said Benson, who was sitting alone on a bar stool, "I hope you will forgive me for seeking you out."

"I'm pleased you did."

"Actually, I usually come in here for lunch on Wednesdays. My Mrs Taylor doesn't come on Wednesdays and so she's not there to cook me lunch as she usually does."

"And Saturdays and Sundays."

"She always leaves me well stocked up after her big bake on Fridays. I fend for myself at weekends. I am fortunate in that respect because this place is packed out for lunch on Saturdays. Wednesdays are slack, of course, because the shops close at one and the town is dead in the afternoon."

"Have a drink, sir. After your splendid hospitality last night. . . ."

"Thank you. The same again, please. Bitter."

The bar was a long, low, attractively-beamed room with a smoke-grimed ceiling and a lot of warm red in its decor—red lamp shades, red cushions on chairs, red terry-towelling place mats on the bar and a turkey red carpet. The bar counter was long, like half a paper-clip split lengthwise, turning back to the wall at each end, leaving just enough room between itself and the side walls for a door—one marked Ladies and the other Gentlemen. It was called "the snug", and it was snug. Several centuries of convivial meeting and drinking had given it an atmosphere that had soaked into the fabric, from which it diffused into the room just as a modern storage heater garners heat only to radiate it into the surrounding air.

The two tankards of bitter arrived.

"You said you had come here to see me, Mr Benson," reminded Masters.

"Because last night I made some suggestions which probably amounted to accusations. I had not expected you, of course, so I had in no way prepared what I said to you then. I believed what I said to be true, and I still believe it to be true. But I was bothered lest I had been intemperate."

"You began to think you had been surprised into making an unprepared statement and so had either misled me or been unjust to those whom we discussed."

"You are an understanding man, Mr Masters. So you will appreciate that I was less than happy when I reviewed our conversation."

"I cannot recall any time when, in my view, you overplayed what you had to say."

"First off, I didn't have to say very much of what I did say. And second, I felt I should have attempted to check my references."

"I can only say I am pleased you spoke as you did. Had you been inhibited, your information would have been of far less use to me and the local police."

"It's kind of you to say so. Nevertheless, when you called this morning I was preparing to set out to do that which I should have done had I known you were intending to call on me last evening."

"You were about to check your references?" asked Masters with a smile.

"Indeed. I said nothing to you about it at the time because I wanted to do my snooping first. If I confirmed that what I had said was not an exaggeration, so much the better. If I found I had gone over the score, I could then seek you out."

"As you have done. Have you discovered that something you said may have been an exaggeration?"

"Far from it. I suspect I have not opened your eyes to all that is going on."

"Ah! Do you wish to tell me now, or later? If now, I would like Green to hear it, too."

"As you wish."

"Why shouldn't the three of us have lunch together? Or why not make it a foursome. Superintendent Frimley is the local man who will need to do the mopping up here after I and mine have gone."

"Very well."

With Benson's consent, Masters beckoned Green over from where he was talking to Frimley.

"Greeny, Mr Benson has something he wishes to tell us. I think Frimley should hear it, too. Could you arrange for a table for the four of us in about ten minutes' time and tell the other three to eat at another table?"

"Pleasure! Nice to see you, Mr Benson. I'll have a word with you at lunch."

Benson nodded, and as Green went away, said to Masters: "Did you find a gimmel flask at Mrs Horbium's?"

"We did. All nice and dusty and unused for years. But a curious thing happened."

"Really. Am I allowed to know what it was?"

"I was surprised to learn that Mrs Horbium, though merely a dilettante collector, was nevertheless unaware of the name gimmel flasks!"

"I must say, I'm a little surprised, too. But she is in no way an academic collector. By that I mean she does not study her subject, except perhaps superficially. She is like a natural singer who can make a passably pleasant sound as an amateur, and so is regarded as a singer, until she is compared with the trained professional. Then her defects become obvious. She is a hobbyist. Nothing more. A hobbyist with a certain amount of natural appreciation of the antique world."

Masters nodded as if to say that Benson had fairly summed up his own opinion of Mrs Horbium's expertise. Then he remarked: "But the curious thing I mentioned happened a moment later when, having said she did not know what a gimmel flask was, she qualified that by saying that the first time she had heard the word gimmel was several weeks ago. Then, as might be expected, she added how very funny it is that having heard a strange word once, one almost invariably heard it a second time shortly afterwards."

"A common remark, but the experience has, nevertheless, happened to all of us in our time, and so we comment on the apparent coincidence, when what we should be acknowledging is that we have been more awake than usual and so have been more alive to the occurrence."

Masters nodded again. "Of course the fact that gimmel flasks had been recently discussed in Limpid—by anybody—was of interest to me."

"Naturally."

"So I asked Mrs Horbium who had spoken to her about them the first time. And her reply was that it was Lamont."

Benson stared in near disbelief. "Now that really does surprise me. The man has no knowledge of and no feeling for the world of antiques. I say this with some certainty, because of late he has made several rather clumsy attempts to pump me on the subject. Indeed, I had come to the conclusion that he was intent upon making a killing in the market because he was in financial difficulties, and was hoping that somehow he might glean from me some hint or tid-bit of information which might enable him to do this."

Masters signalled for more beer.

"You say you got that impression solely from his showing eagerness to make money in a sphere which he patently knew nothing about? Or were there other reasons which helped bring you to that conclusion?"

"It is always difficult to say with strict accuracy how, when and why an idea entered one's head. But I must confess that I have no knowledge whatsoever of Lamont's financial state."

"But?"

The beer arrived. Benson waited until the barman was out of earshot before replying.

"One of the saddest things in life, to my way of thinking, is to see the man who has married fairly young and who then gets on in life—either financially or socially—outgrow his wife: leave her behind because she cannot keep up or, in some cases, actually grow ashamed of her."

"You think that this is what has happened in Lamont's case?"

Benson smoothed his grey hair with one hand, as though considering his reply, lest he be guilty of the hastiness he believed he might have shown the previous evening.

"I will not say so categorically. But I will give it as my opinion that this is so. Mrs Lamont had an animal attraction in her youth. She came from a home where her mother cared little and her father less. To survive she had to be strong and, I believe, physically proud. Does that term surprise you?"

"Not in the least. I would have called it physical arrogance, perhaps, but I recognise your description. I have never seen Mrs Lamont, but I feel I can visualise her. A strong body, marching proud, heels put down firmly, back straight, nose in the air, brows straight across the forehead. I'd guess at dark hair and a severish or simple line in clothes. How am I doing so far?"

"A verbal photograph. It's uncanny. She was an apprentice hairdresser. She could sometimes be seen going on some errand on the market hill, wearing a white overall which she tightened in at the waist with a black belt. She almost shouldered her way through crowds, looking at nobody, as aloof as only somebody with an arrogant spirit and a consciousness of her own physical power could be. Unfortunately her face is the sort that, once it had lost its early youth, coarsened into what I would call a bad tempered heaviness which has the remnants of form one would expect to find more in a man who has run-to-seed than in a woman."

"And is it your opinion that Lamont is now no longer attracted to her?"

"I imagine that might have happened whatever his success or failure in business. But Lamont over the past few years has made a deal of easy money. Now, I can't answer for his attitude, but appearances would suggest that his wife believes in the old tag 'easy come, easy go'. Or, if I am doing her an injustice there, then I think she is compensating for what she didn't have in youth. She has her own big car. They have a big house and a cruiser on the river, and they live in a style to match. Need I go on?"

"I think not. Her expensive tastes may well mean that Lamont is feeling a financial draught. But could it not be that her over-compensation in over-spending may be due to her disappointment at her husband's attitude? If he no longer cares, or is running other women. . . ?"

"I had considered that, but I have no knowledge of other women in his life."

"Rumour, perhaps?"

"Faint. But I have no details."

"Would it surprise you to learn that when Mrs Horbium heard Lamont mention gimmel flasks, he was in the company of Joanna Wellerby? He was apparently spending the evening at her cottage."

There was a short silence. Masters broke it.

"You haven't answered my question, Mr Benson."

"And you, being the man you are, will be drawing conclusions from my silence?"

"You must agree that silence in response to a bombshell denotes either shock or a strong desire not to comment because the explosion lays bare some knowledge the hearer had previously covered."

"In this case," said Benson quietly, "it is both. The thought of a woman like Joanna Wellerby consorting with Lamont is distasteful. Unaesthetic. Lamont is greasy. Literally, I believe."

"I don't know the man, but Green has described him to me in far from complimentary terms."

"I'm sure he has. Your colleague has a pungent turn of phrase."

"So I can assume that this association caused the shock part of the reaction. What about the other?"

"Joanna Wellerby was brought up in Limpid, as I was. Of course I am nearly twenty years older than she is, but she was known to us because of her well publicised ability as a pianist even in her teens. By then I was married, and when we came home on leave, my wife and I usually returned here to stay with my parents. So my wife got to know people here. She got to know the young Joanna. My wife's name for her was 'the fast young lady'."

"Meaning what exactly?"

"The more discerning of our womenfolk have an instinct about their sisters. I trusted my wife's wisdom. What she intended to convey by those words was her belief that sooner or later, because of her uninhibited attitude towards men, young Joanna would cause disaster or discord of some sort. She was good-looking, talented, spoilt and possessed of a power over males which, from the age of sixteen, she exercised up to, and beyond, the point of discretion."

"Go on."

"She married Wellerby, whom I do not know and have never met."

"From whom she is now separated."

"I hadn't seen Joanna for so long that when I

caught a glimpse of her two months ago, in Mrs Horbium's company, I could not recall her identity, though the face was familiar. A day or so later, before I could remember who she was, I was told her name and given the information that she and her husband were separated. My wife's predictions came back so strongly to me over the years, that I asked an acquaintance of mine in London, who does know Wellerby, what the circumstances were under which they had parted."

"You got to know?"

"My information is that it was Wellerby who left Joanna. Reports are said to have reached him, concerning Joanna's behaviour on her foreign tours, that would have caused any man to leave any woman. As it was, I understand, Wellerby stuck it longer than most could have managed. Finally, after some sort of trouble in Belgium, he threw in his hand. He left her. She came down here."

"Surely a strange place for a woman of her supposed reputation to bury herself."

"Not if she needed to play for time for some reason or to drop out while something died down."

"You may be right. Meanwhile she is contenting herself with Lamont. Her choice of man shocked you, but not the fact that she is still playing the part of the fast young lady?"

Benson nodded. "It is amazing how a conversation should get round to topics which are often totally unconnected with your investigation."

"Conversations always veer off the main subject. Now, I think we should eat. There's more conversation to come, and I'm anxious to hear it."

*　　*　　*

"The dish of the day," said Green, "is liver pudding. Can anybody please enlighten me as to what liver pudding is?" He looked up from the menu at Frimley, who shrugged his shoulders.

"I don't think there's much mystery," said Benson. "It is an excellent dish. Substitute liver cut very small for the steak and kidney in a pudding, and you have the answer. The chef here does know what he's doing, gentlemen. He uses onions and, I suspect, strips of bacon. If you are seeking a recommendation, I am prepared to supply it."

"In that case," said Masters, "I'll have the pudding."

The others followed his lead. The waiter brought the trolley round. The puddings had been cooked in stone jam jars which were perfectly cylindrical with no narrowing at the neck. When he saw them, Green exclaimed: "I'll say the chef knows his stuff! My old mother always steamed puddings in jam jars like that. We used to get them with plum jam in. Three pounders. You could use those jars for anything. Wonderful. Bag blue in one, scraps of soap in another, pickled onions in a dozen of them, red cabbage . . . the list was endless. Stone jars! They're antiques today, aren't they, Mr Benson?"

"There is a certain vogue for them, and the old pop bottles with a glass ball in the neck, flat irons . . . all the things that were everyday items when we were young, Mr Green."

Green accepted half of a complete pudding. The other three had one between them. For a time there was silence as they ate. Benson's eyes were twinkling as he looked around. The others, in turn, nodded approbation as they felt his eye on them and looked up.

"You know what," said Green, "I can't think why I've never come across this before. Succulent. I like offal."

Masters looked across at Benson. "Now, sir. You have something to tell us, I believe."

Benson laid down his knife and fork.

"I went out this morning to emulate you. Investigating. I am, you see, very interested in the buildings in Limpid. My family has lived hereabouts for generations and I'm fond of the place. Too fond of it to want to see wholesale destruction to make way for modern nightmare buildings. In the last six months there has been a move in the local council to have one side of the market hill demolished to make way for supermarkets and multi-storey car parks. You know the sort of thing—entirely characterless and duplicated in every urban centre in the country."

"Hang on a moment," interrupted Frimley. "I've heard something about this. Benson! Of course. You're the one who started a petition against demolition and got over three thousand signatures."

"That's right. Specifically to help Theraby, the man who keeps the outfitter's on the hill. One of those good, old-fashioned shops that stocks all the little things like studs and braces and buttons and reach-me-down trousers. The sort of merchandise a modern shop would never think of stocking. He was told to expect a compulsory purchase order."

"Has he got it yet?" asked Green.

"No. Frederick Hardy was a councillor. He fought it."

"That's something in his favour."

"One might think so. His office is just above Theraby's shop and although he had not received any hint that it would be taken, he made no secret of the fact that he was fighting the development plan in his own interests, lest the plan should be expanded to include his office."

"That was fairly open dealing at any rate."

"I think not."

"Ah!" Masters leant forward. "Hanky panky?"

"I believe so."

"You've got a very good reason for saying that?"

"I spent this morning asking questions."

"Go on."

"Hardy was a natural to be appointed to the planning committee, because of his business interests. He was a professional among amateurs—except for one other councillor. Stephen Yorkwall is a builder in a biggish way."

"I know him," said Frimley. "Never had any dealings with him. But from what I hear he wouldn't like to be called a builder. He's managing director of a construction company."

"I'm pleased you mentioned that. I shall return to the point later. But for the moment, may I just say that one of my acquaintances in Limpid is the town clerk. Augustus Frane, besides being a solicitor, is an amateur historian and the author of a very pleasantly written history of Limpid. His interests and mine converge when any local find is made, as sometimes happens. So this morning, for the first time in our friendship, I presumed to call on him in his office. I had a ready-made excuse to broach the subject of the market hill development scheme, because as you have heard, I made it my business to organise the petition opposing it."

"Frane, being an historian, would be against it himself, I suppose," murmured Masters.

"Oh, quite. But as a servant of the council he obviously had to remain neutral, and he was very correct. But when two old friends meet . . . well, to cut the story short, I asked him point blank who had first put forward the idea of the market hill development."

"I take it that this time he was not quite so neutral or correct as formerly?" asked Masters.

"Shall we say he left me in no doubt that Yorkwall was the instigator. Frane said that Yorkwall had delineated his scheme with great exactitude and laughingly gave the reason for doing so. It was, he stated, so that his old colleague Hardy wouldn't feel the draught."

"By that I take it he meant he proposed that the area involved should not include Hardy's office, but start just below it and extend some way down the hill," said Masters.

"Quite. But had he included Hardy's office building he might have been more successful in steering his plan through the committee."

"How come?" asked Green.

"Because, as the scheme did not involve Hardy's office, it meant that Hardy was free to argue against it. Had he been involved, he would have been an interested party and, as such, would not have been allowed to speak and vote without declaring his interest—if at all—which would almost certainly have robbed his protest of its sting."

"And Hardy was instrumental in getting the scheme scrapped?"

"That is common knowledge. It is said he went all

out against it because he feared he would suffer eventually."

"It is said? You don't think that is true?"

"I think Yorkwall is too wily a bird not to have nobbled Hardy by including his office, had he, Yorkwall, really wanted his scheme to succeed."

"Are you saying that the whole affair was a charade played out by Hardy and Yorkwall in collusion, to fool local opinion and fellow councillors?"

"I believe so."

"What causes you to believe so, Mr Benson?"

The waiter arrived to take orders for second courses. It gave Benson a moment or two in which to marshall his thoughts. He seemed to need them. Masters got the impression that Benson was basically, at this moment, an angry man. A fair-minded man angered by knowledge of foul play and prepared to make use of the opportunity their presence offered him to help put matters to rights. Who for? For Limpid? For his friends like Theraby the shopkeeper?

As if reading Masters' thoughts, Benson said: "I have, as you know, a number of friends in trade and business on the market hill. They are people whom I pass the time of day with most days. Among them is a mutual friend of Frane and myself. My bank manager. His bank, the East Anglian, is cheek by jowl with the little shops on the hill, and stands not far above the Corn Exchange. Whilst we were talking, Frane, who must really be suffering from a sense of divided loyalties over this business, suggested that I should have a word with Kettle—the bank manager. Kettle is a quiet little man. But a thinker! He plays chess well, and he has a sense of humour. He has, in his time, contributed to *Punch*. The burden of his humour is usually bureaucracy and government. He is out of sympathy with both."

"Did Frane suggest why you should talk to Kettle?"

"No. And I pride myself I was wise enough not to ask him. I guessed he was going to let Kettle be his mouthpiece—knowing Kettle's antipathy for many of the unsavoury dealings of today, I know Frane felt sure that Kettle would speak out."

"Kettle gave you something that made you think?"

Benson nodded and waited until his sweet had been set in front of him before continuing.

"As Mr Frimley will know, quite recently there has been a merger between our two local eastern counties banks—supposedly in the interests of economy. I knew this before I called on Kettle. It is common knowledge and has been reported in the press. Branches of both banks—the East Anglian and the British Woollen—are to be found in every sizeable town south of Lincoln and east of the Trent. But what I did not know, before Kettle told me, was that in each town one or other of the branches is to go, and in Limpid it is Kettle's East Anglian that is being disposed of.

"When I asked to see him and Kettle very kindly received me, I told him Frane had suggested I should speak to him about the possibility of buildings on that side of the hill being demolished. Knowing of my active interest in the matter, Kettle rather let his hair down. I said that I found the disposal of the bank an amazing thing. After all, there would still be as much business to transact as ever—probably more if the merger produced the increased business that was expected. Kettle was very bitter about it. Not only is the number of banks to be halved, but the number of managers, too—for obvious reasons. The banks that remain open are to have their staffs slightly increased by members of the staffs from the banks that are being closed down."

"So your pal, Kettle, is redundant, is he?" asked Green.

Benson nodded. "At fifty-five. A difficult age for such a man to find employment. He was despondent when I arrived."

"As well as bitter?" asked Green.

"When you arrived? Had he cheered up by the time you left him?" asked Frimley.

"Considerably. I was able to give him an introduction to an acquaintance of mine with a small firm who feels the need for an executive to deal with tax matters. He wants either a civil servant from the Treasury or a bank official. Kettle should suit him admirably."

"As a result of your introduction," said Masters, "did Mr Kettle grow a little indiscreet?"

"He told me that his bank building is to be sold and is already under offer to. . . ."

"To whom?"

I was told in the greatest confidence—and I hope this will remain confidential—that a property company called Goodwerry were hoping to buy."

"Never heard the name," said Green.

"Neither had I until that moment. And then, like Mrs Horbium and her gimmel flask, I heard it again very shortly afterwards."

"Go on."

"I dropped in on my friends the Racines. In response to a few questions from me I discovered that six weeks ago they had learned that their camera shop, which they rent, had been acquired from its former owner by a property company called Goodwerry."

"The devil, it was."

"I called on Theraby, too. He, I know, owns his own property as his father owned it before him, so there could be no question of Goodwerry having bought the freehold unbeknown to him. But Goodwerry had been active."

Masters said: "I believe I can guess the form their activity took. They approached Theraby with the assurance that though the move to purchase his property compulsorily had failed this time, the plan would not be dropped. Sooner, rather than later, the business will come up again, and next time it will not fail. They pointed out that these days the individual never wins against authority in the long run. They hinted that Theraby had a year, perhaps two, before he is closed down."

Benson smiled. "Your guess is remarkably accurate. What was the object of their approach, do you suppose?"

"To point out that all property under the threat of compulsory purchase is virtually worthless. Particularly a business. Not only would nobody buy it, but the goodwill would be demolished with the building. All Theraby could hope to get for such a poor old building would be a meagre recompense decided by those who only wanted it to destroy it. But Goodwerry were prepared to help him. They would pay him a fair price for the property as a gamble which he, as a man in a small way of business, could not af-

ford to take. In other words, they tried to persuade
him to sell."

"Quite right."

"Has Theraby agreed to sell?"

"He is seriously considering the offer."

"Was that the end of your investigation?"

"Not quite. Bessie at the dairy tells me she has a
new landlord, too."

"Goodwerry?"

"Goodwerry."

"What do you make of it all, Mr Benson?"

"I was hoping that you would be in a position to
have the register of companies yield some of its
secrets—such as discovering the names of the people
who constitute Goodwerry."

"That can be done. You are expecting the names
to be . . . interesting?"

"Aren't you?"

"Frankly, yes!"

"Then that, gentlemen, is my tale. Whether it
helps you in any way in your present investigation, I
do not know. But having learned what I did, I was in
no doubt that I should speak to you of it."

Frimley answered. "We're grateful, Mr Benson. We
none of us know what the result of this conversation
may turn out to be. But rest assured we shall do whatever may be necessary about this business."

"Thank you. In that case, gentlemen, I will bid you
good afternoon."

Benson flicked his fingers for his bill and rose stiffly
to his feet. The three detectives sat silent for a few
moments.

"I could go a cup of coffee," announced Green, signalling to the waiter. "Anybody else?" He took a packet of Kensitas from his pocket and offered it to Frimley, who refused.

Frimley tapped the table pensively after agreeing to allow the waiter to put a coffee cup in front of him and fill it.

"Come on, Wally," urged Masters. "Out with it."

"This chap Benson. How far can we trust him? We seem to be accepting his word without any form of checking. I don't like it."

"Quite right, too. But don't forget I did check on him overnight."

"All you got was a character reference. You got nothing to indicate that he couldn't be implicated in some local shenanigan, or that he isn't just using us in the hope of paying off old scores against people he doesn't like."

"I'd go even further," said Masters with a smile. "He's an intelligent man, and we have to consider whether all the chat he's given us is not just a part of some gigantic smoke screen he is putting up to shield himself or his friends from our murder investigation. While listening to what he says, I have that very much in the forefront of my mind. For instance, were he not lame and consequently a very slow mover, I'd be considering whether or not he could have dodged in and out of those bushes in the Pellucid House garden, and Greeny here would be going over the ground looking for holes made by his stick."

"There weren't any of those," confessed Frimley. "We combed those grounds on Sunday and Monday and I can assure you there were no holes made by walking sticks."

"Excellent. But there's one other thing I am bearing in mind. *Croton Tiglium,* the plant from which croton oil seeds come, is grown in Africa, India, South America and the far eastern tropical islands. Benson was a foreign service man, and got about the world quite a bit at the Monarch's expense. I have not lost sight of the fact that he could have imported either the seeds or the oil during his service days, and has now used them."

"It would explain why we haven't been able to trace the source."

"The only other person among those whom we have met so far who appears to be a traveller is Joanna Wellerby. Whether her concerts have taken her to areas where she could pick up croton oil seeds is a matter for doubt. But the fact must be remembered."

"Okay," said Frimley, "so you're on the ball and have not lost sight of Benson, but I'm still wary of trusting him too far."

"Quite right, mate," rejoined Green. "And the first chance we get, we'll check him out."

"You'll get that chance, I hope, this afternoon," said Masters.

"How?" asked Frimley, glumly. "By going along to the friends he's already primed and asking them just the questions he's programmed us to ask?"

"Hardly," grinned Masters. "Come on, Wally, think! Benson told his story with a lot of background detail. Detail which seemingly corroborates it and made it sound genuine. Think of something he said which can be checked independently."

"I've been trying."

"In that case, try this. Benson said Theraby had been approached by Goodwerry—had been urged to sell to them. We got to know the type of approach they made. We also learned that the camera shop and the dairy had changed hands. Goodwerry is now the owner. Why don't we approach the former owners and discover what it was that had caused them to sell so suddenly? If we get to know that they were subjected to the same pressure as Theraby, would that not confirm—in part at least—what we have heard from Benson?"

Frimley looked up and grinned sheepishly. "I should have thought of that for myself. The indirect approach! Everybody can't be in a conspiracy with Benson."

"If you approve, Wally, I'd like Greeny and Colin Hoame to take on that chore this afternoon. The land registry or whatever they call it locally—or possibly the local rates department—will tell them who the former owners were, and they can pursue the matter from there."

"How is this likely to further the murder investigation?"

"I honestly don't know. But I think we have to stir up all the dirt and then wait for the water to clear again. You never know, we may find a motive somewhere in the mud."

"Them's my sentiments, too," said Green. "There's a stink round here, and Hardy's murder is only part of it. But I definitely reckon it is part of it. It was the first whiff we got and it's leading us to the midden."

Frimley got to his feet.

"What you propose, George, suits me fine. Greeny has his job. What's ours?"

"I'll ring London and ask for a run-down on Good-werry."

"That suits me. I think I ought to call Telford. I can do that while you're at the station ringing London."

Masters nodded his agreement and turned to Green. "I shall need a bit of light reading while I'm waiting for the Yard to check up on Goodwerry. Could I have those catalogues young Berger picked up this morning? I'd like to glance through them to see what is sold at the auctions."

"You can have the lot. Invoices and all. You never know, something may click and need crosschecking. I'll tell Berger to get them for you."

After putting in his call to the Yard, Masters wandered into the interview room which had been put at his disposal as a temporary office. He threw the catalogues and invoice books on the table and sat down.

He had now been in Limpid for almost twenty-four hours, and though he was far from dissatisfied with the progress he had made, he was very aware of the fact that the police—if he counted the local crime squad's not inconsiderable efforts before he arrived— had been on the job for three whole days, without turning up any information that could point the investigation in any one particular direction. This worried him slightly, because as Green had told Telford he was a firm believer in the old saying in CID that the mystery which isn't cracked inside forty-eight hours may well turn out to be very protracted indeed. Always he had striven to have some idea of the direction of search he should take at the earliest possible

moment. He didn't worry whether the indicator involved means, motive, method or opportunity. They
were all invariably interlinked—a vicious circle into
which he could break at any point, and from there
proceed to wind up the case. But here in Limpid he
felt he had not broken in. He knew how the murder
had been committed and what with. Those facts had
been handed to him on a plate. They did not form
part of the circle. Nor could he honestly believe that
Mrs Hardy, the nearest relative of the victim—that
good old first objective of investigating officers—was in
any way implicated. But was that a good enough reason for not looking at her harder than had been done
so far? Hardy might have alienated his wife over the
years to the point where she might now think she
would be a happier woman with him dead. She
would certainly not have to live in penury, and if
Hardy were to have a sizeable life insurance to add to
Pellucid House and its contents and whatever share
of the auctioneering business would revert to her
. . . he made a mental note to get Reed to look
into the business of insurance. Dammit! He'd forgotten that most estate agents and auctioneers ran an insurance agency, too. Hardy, as an agent, would have
had a good chance of getting a big policy on favoura-
ble terms.

He felt the need to tighten up the investigation.
He had foolishly allowed himself to be pressured by
Telford into becoming a tutor for the local officers,
and their presence had denied him the opportunity
for much of his usual inspirational approach. He had
been trying so hard to play it by the book and to go
through all the motions for the sake of Frimley and

Hoame that he had not taken the opportunity to leap out here and there and to cut corners elsewhere.

He sadly regretted his suggestion of the previous day that he should saddle himself with Frimley and Hoame just to pander to Telford's local pride.

CHAPTER VII

Masters had looked through the catalogue of the sale which had been postponed, and the April sale at which the twenty-seven pieces of glassware had been sold, before the outside phone rang. He had no idea what he was looking for, if anything, but he was never one to do things by halves, and having decided to look through the catalogues, he was doing the job thoroughly. The call, when it came, was an unwelcome interruption. He was enjoying his excursion into areas hitherto unknown to him.

The information from the Yard was definite and concise. The Goodwerry Property Company was a bare six months old. It had been floated with a nominal capital of one thousand pounds put up in two equal parcels of five hundred each by nominees. These nominees were the East Anglian Bank, who were also bankers for the company. East Anglian had been asked to divulge the names of the shareholders and had done so under protest. The shareholders were Thomas Edward Yorkwall, builder, of Limpid and Kevin Moorhouse Williams, chartered auctioneer and surveyor, also of Limpid. The registered office was number 11 Corrector Place, London, W.2.

Masters thanked his informant and replaced the phone. Yorkwall he had expected—as had Benson. But Williams, no! Williams—the partner whom nobody had mentioned. The dark horse? Hardy, the senior partner, was dead. Lamont, the junior partner, was in financial trouble. Williams, the middle partner, had not so far merited discussion. Why? How had it happened that attention had been diverted from him?

It was while Masters was putting these questions to himself that Telford, followed by Frimley, entered the interview room.

"Hello, sir. I hadn't expected to see you this afternoon," said Masters.

"To tell you the truth, I hadn't expected to be here. But I came over to hear Frimley's report in full because—well, quite frankly, the murder case is a sort of nine days' wonder as far as we're concerned, but widespread corruption, if it exists, is likely to be a headache to us for a long time. And where you'll deal with the murder and then go off back to London, we shall have the other business on our own plate for long enough."

Masters nodded to show he understood why Telford should attach more importance to the corruption problem than to the murder case.

"I've heard what Wally has had to tell me," went on Telford, "and it poses all sorts of problems."

"None of it is entirely proven as yet."

"Maybe not. But there's too much circumstantial evidence for it to be a complete mare's nest. Wally told me you'd checked out on Benson, and I'm prepared to accept what he says if you are."

"For the time being."

"Of course. But if only one tenth of what he says is true, there's going to be an upheaval here. And quite frankly I'm not looking forward to it. When the police start tangling with local government it's unsavoury."

"Agreed."

"So what I came in to say," went on Telford, his pale face sweating under the ordeal, "is to ask for your help in getting a pretty quick solution to this local scandal."

"I'm only here for the murder."

"I know. But it's your preliminary investigations into the murder that have started this business, so I was wondering if, as you go on investigating the murder, you would do what you can to unearth information about the local scandal."

"Of course. Always willing to help. And to show willing, here is the first tidbit. The Goodwerry Property Company is owned jointly by Councillor Yorkwall and Kevin Williams, Hardy's partner."

"Williams?" The surprise in Frimley's tone matched the surprise Masters had felt on first hearing the name. "Williams? Not Hardy?"

Telford who, so far, had remained standing, now sat down heavily. "Yorkwall and Williams, eh? Well, your pal Benson suggested that if we got the names of the Goodwerry set up we might also get a surprise, but do you reckon he thought Williams and not Hardy had joined up with Yorkwall?"

"I think not."

"But this corroborates part of his story," said

Telford. "It could mean he's given us a straight story in general, if not in detail."

"No, no," insisted Frimley. "If it's Williams and not Hardy on the Goodwerry board, it makes a nonsense of Benson's suggestion that Yorkwall and Hardy's caperings in the planning committee were a show put on by them to fool people."

Masters shook his head. "Sorry, Wally. Hardy may not have been a knowing partner to the charade, but I'm sure he played the part he was cast for. Yorkwall and Williams knew how he would react, so they left out the H.W. and L. offices to leave Hardy free to do just what was expected of him. And he did it to their satisfaction."

"To what real end?"

"To devalue the market hill property. Yorkwall and Williams don't want the council to build there any more than you do. But they wanted to create an atmosphere of fear and doubt among the property owners there. The fear that the plan would come up a second time and succeed. So the owners would be prepared to sell at almost any price, and think themselves lucky to get a buyer. But Yorkwall, who had instigated the first plan, knew he would never resurrect it. The property owners didn't know that. Didn't know the whole thing was a con. So Goodwerry has bought some of the most valuable commercial property in Limpid at knock-down prices. I wonder how long it will be before the rents are raised above what the present occupiers can afford?"

"It's a smart trick," said Telford. "Nobody can get at either Yorkwall or Williams for it."

"Why not?" asked Frimley.

"Yorkwall is free to suggest what he likes in

Council. He didn't own any of the property concerned at the time. Nothing there to get him for. Hardy fought the scheme. I imagine he did it off his own bat, but even if Williams did do a bit of gentle prodding, how are we to prove it with Hardy dead? After the collapse of the scheme—and only after its collapse—Yorkwall and Williams move in and buy. Nothing illegal there. What do you say, Mr Masters?"

"I see your point, sir, but I'd go out to get them on conspiracy to defraud. If the former owners all tell the same story about the way Goodwerry approached them—the way Theraby was approached—then you may have them. An independent valuation of the property will establish just how much below its worth the owners were offered, and accepted."

"That's right," said Frimley, "and if you do nothing else, you show the locals what sort of men these two are, and they'll be finished hereabouts."

"I wish I could believe that," rejoined Telford. "The ungodly flourish all too often for my liking."

Telford had called for a pot of tea to be brought to the interview room, and the three of them were drinking it and still talking.

"I've been interested to hear," Telford said to Masters, "that you've been concentrating on finding or tracing that flask. Why's that? I'd like to hear an expert's reason for making a choice like that."

Masters shrugged. "Where do you start any murder investigation such as this which isn't of the instant material clue variety? There are no fingerprints, no bloodstained weapons, no obvious suspects to get to work on. In this case you handed me the name of a poison and described a method of delivery. You then spent from Sunday afternoon until yesterday afternoon looking for the source of the poison. Your search was countrywide and thorough and yet unprofitable. I'd have been rather silly not to accept what you had discovered—that there is no readily apparent source of the poison. So I am left with a description of the means of delivery. That took place at Limpid at lunchtime on Sunday. So I stood a better chance of learning more about it, even if I couldn't locate it, than I did of tracing the poison. So I started there, on as many fronts as possible. Some of the stuff we've dredged up may prove useful."

"I see. You haven't a single suspect, though, have you?"

"No."

"That's honest at any rate."

"What's the use of blinking facts? In no time at all I could have too many suspects. No human endeavour is ever perfect. But having said that, are you dissatisfied with what the last twenty-four hours have produced."

"Not dissatisfied. But I don't like it. I feel tensed up, waiting for something to break."

"I know the feeling. . . ."

Whatever else Masters was about to say was interrupted by a knock on the door and Green came in, followed by Hoame, Reed and Berger.

"Any tea left?" asked Green feeling the pot with both hands.

"Get some more," suggested Frimley.

"Any news?" asked Masters.

Green looked across at him. "We've seen three former owners. They all tell the same story. Goodwerry told them the council would try again, but offered to take the property off their hands because they, Goodwerry, being a big company, could fight the council better than individual owners. So they got the goods at their own price."

Masters asked Frimley: "Is that good enough for you to work on?"

"And to prove Benson right? Yes."

"What are you going to do?" Telford asked his subordinate.

"Right this moment, sir, nothing. I was hoping we could clear the decks of the Hardy murder first, perhaps gathering a few more facts about the corruption as we go, and then we can make a full-blooded assault. I'd rather have the advice of some of the Documents Squad when I get to grips with it, sir."

"Is that how you'd play it?" Telford asked Masters.

"It seems as reasonable as any other. But I must admit I'd be so scared of a corruption investigation. . . ."

"You?"

"Yes, him," said Green. "In the car coming down here he was looking as glum as hell because he sniffed corruption in the air."

"Now you *are* pulling my leg," said Telford. "There was no hint of corruption until you stumbled on it last night."

"Mr Green's right, sir," said Berger. "We all heard it in the car, didn't we sarge?"

Appealed to, Reed nodded. "True enough."

"He had enough . . . what's the word . . . prescience to know there'd be corruption?"

"You've heard the lads," repled Green.

"Please," said Masters. "I think it was your signal to the Yard that did it. All about wealthy estate agents and local councillors. They've been in the news a lot lately. It was just association of ideas on my part."

"Some association!" said Hoame, impressed.

Masters, who liked admiration as much as any man, grinned at him. "We're a nasty, suspicious lot at the Yard. Greeny invariably thinks the worst of everybody, and I think the worst of everything. That way we cover the whole field and so we're never surprised."

"I've noticed."

"Have you?" Masters turned to Reed. "What about Hardy's life insurance?"

"No joy there, Chief. I made three visits. To Hardy's solicitor, his accountant, and that plummy chief clerk of his. They all told me that Hardy had just the one insurance on his own life—for about five thousand. He took it out years ago before he really struck it rich. The chief clerk told me that since he'd made money Hardy had said he could see no point in taking out more as Mrs Hardy would be well provided for in any case. It appears she had a modest policy on her old man's life, and I enquired whether he'd taken a mortgage on his house in an endowment policy, but he hadn't. He'd bought outright because he was too old when he bought it to get an endowment."

"That settles that, then. Thank you, sergeant." Masters looked across at Telford. "Just checking to see Hardy hadn't got a thumping great policy which could prove a motive for his murder."

"I'm pleased you're leaving no loopholes. That lets his missus out, does it, in your opinion?"

"Shall we say it gives us no reason to concentrate on her to the exclusion of everybody else."

"So now what? Or haven't you planned your next move?"

Masters felt annoyed at this question. He planned when it was necessary, but when he had a capful of information, he liked to think things over or, alternatively, play it as it came. It was the difference between flair and routine in police work. The difference between the flier and the plodder. The creative instinct versus the pedestrian approach. All his annoyance with himself—and Telford—for having agreed to accept Frimley and Hoame as students came flooding back. Their presence held him back. It was like carrying two buckets of sand. He preferred to work in private. In public he felt the need to explain his actions—felt it was expected of him—and he couldn't. His mind was too busy with the problem to divert itself into explanatory channels. The arrangement was a burden to him: an annoying burden. But he kept calm, knowing that to show edginess now would be taken as a sign of weakness or a crack in his carapace of ability. So his answer when it came was mild enough, but shocking.

"I've planned my next move, all right. I'm going to buy a tin of tobacco. Oh! And some matches. On the High Street."

Telford stared for a moment.

"And these others?"

An imp of mischief leapt into Masters' brain.

"Sir, you are putting your foot in it."

"Me? How?"

"Your two officers are co-operating with us for our

mutual benefit, but chiefly to see how a Yard team works."

"Yes."

"We place great importance on initiative. If I had to tell everybody in my team every move to make, every thought to think, I might as well do it all myself."

"You mean you don't know what to tell them to do."

"I mean I have no need to tell them. Wally here, has already realised that a new factor has now crept in. I refer to Williams. So far he has been overlooked. Wally knows that he, as the local man, is the one most suited to go out and get us a complete run down on Williams: his financial state, his love life, his hopes, his fears, his actions—in fact, everything there is to be known about the man and his family."

Telford turned to Frimley. "Is that right?"

Frimley, not averse to playing Masters' game, replied: "That is on my list, sir. But before I do that I want to visit Mrs Hardy and ask her what visitors she has had for meals lately. I was wondering, you see, whether I couldn't get a lead as to who might have seen that flask in use. I can probably narrow it down, because I don't suppose Mrs Hardy puts on a salad every time she has guests."

"I get your drift," said Masters. "Bear in mind that the flask has probably been more in evidence since his doctor told Hardy to cut down on the carbohydrates."

Telford, still not fully convinced by Masters' ploy asked: "And Green?"

"I've still got a flask to trace," replied Green. "But apart from that I'm going to try and establish where each one of about half a dozen people was at the critical time on Sunday. I mean to say, if somebody we have our eye on was lunching in a road-house fifty miles away, he could hardly have whipped that flask off Hardy's table, could he? So we could forget him. The time has come, you see, to try and eliminate a few people from our reckoning. It's called narrowing the field."

Telford didn't appear to relish Green's tone, but he couldn't argue with the content. So, sticking to his guns, he returned to Masters and asked: "And what about you? Apart from buying tobacco and matches."

Masters grinned.

"The time has come for me to have a think. I've got to get to grips with croton oil. I have a feeling that this particular dose of poison is of great antiquity. A museum strain, perhaps."

"What the hell are you talking about?"

"You're not with me? You must remember the articles in our journals some years back—probably about the time of the Tutankhamun exhibition or just before—when researchers found that they could grow wheat from the grains which had been stored in tombs thousands of years old, and that they could culture bacteria of the same age. They found that the bacteria were resistant to penicillin, which in turn meant that they had been subjected to penicillin treatment in those days, thousands of years before the penicillin era. Museum strains they called them. I've a feeling our croton oil could well be among them. Still active after many years."

Telford was still plainly perplexed, but he murmured something about seeing the point, and got to his feet. Masters looked round the assembled company as if to indicate the meeting was over and people could now get back to business. As a more definite signal, he said to Reed, "When Mr Frimley has finished with you, you'll find me here or—if it's after six, at the pub."

As everybody left, Masters ostentatiously straightened the catalogues and invoice books on the desk and then looked up at Telford, who was hanging back. "Where's the best tobacconist in town?"

"On the High Street," said Telford, and left the interview room rather abruptly.

Masters was not the man to run out of Warlock Flake within twenty-four hours of leaving London, and he had his doubts as to whether a Limpid tobacconist would stock it. But having announced his intentions, he had to go through the motions. He enjoyed the little walk. The weather was what gardeners refer to as open. A mild day, not sunny and hot and sticky. He was interested in the buildings: the library, the masonic lodge, the Oddfellows' Hall, a statue of a man pointing heavenwards to show where all the verdigris had come from . . . and then the tobacconist's. A real tobacconist's, that sold nothing but smokers' requirements, with scores of samples of tobacco on show and the stock stored on shelves in highly glazed, royal blue, swag-bellied urns with burnt-in gilt labels.

Masters request for Warlock Flake caused no surprise. The shopkeeper just produced it. As the man put the brassy tin with its black sphinx logo into a bag, Masters, who was the only customer in the shop, said: "Those tobacco jars. Are they valuable? They look to be very old, and in an area like this where antiques are snapped up, I'd have thought that an array like that would have attracted covetous glances, if not offers to buy."

"Oh, they do, sir. Lots of people would like my gallipots."

"So they're gallipots are they? Do you know, I always thought gallipots were chemists' ware. I suppose I had some hazy idea they were named after Galen."

"A common error, sir. Gallipots can be spelt *galley pots* and mean what they say. Originally, they were literally pots brought to this country in galleys from the Mediterranean. It's true a lot of them were glazed pots and were used by the old apothecaries for storing ointments."

"You've made a study of them?"

"I've learned a bit about them sir—purely in self defence."

"Because of nosey-parkers like me asking about them?"

"Oh no, sir. I don't mind questions. It's people who try to get me to sell. They come in here and say: 'You've got twenty pots there. I'll give you a fiver apiece for them. A hundred quid cash. What d'you say?' "

"And what do you say?"

"Simply that it would cost me more than a hundred pounds to buy new storage jars, so not only would I be out of pocket on the deal, I'd have lost my gallipots, too. Some people really have no idea."

"So what are they worth?"

"Those particular specimens? I've no idea, sir. But they're worth far more to me up there on my shelves than I'd get for them from a dealer. You see, they're not really uncommon. At one time they were made in highly decorated forms, and became known as painted pots. Those made in this country were usually cobalt blue—just like mine are. They're individually thrown of course, so no two are exactly alike, and they're tin glazed—not lead. But as I was saying, there were a lot of the more highly ornamented ones with angels, cherubs and birds on them. Some had cartouches or scrolls on them with the date of manufacture in them. Now those are valuable. And I tell you what I have got, round the back. One or two with pipe-smoker finials."

"Very appropriate," said Masters. "Well, thank you very much for the tobacco and the information. I hope my questions didn't bother you."

"Not at all, sir. And if you can't ask questions—a man in your profession—who can?" The man smiled up at him. "Yes, I know who you are. Not many things are kept secret in Limpid."

"No? Tell me, do you know why I'm here?"

"Looking into the death of Fred Hardy, aren't you?"

"How did he die?"

"Are you asking me?"

"Yes. If nothing is kept secret for long in Limpid, how do people say he died?"

"Poisoned. Wasn't he?"

"Yes he was. What with?"

The man stared hard at Masters. "Ah! Now I've heard various things. Some say arsenic, some say weedkiller and some say it was just severe food poisoning. But what it really was doesn't seem to be known. They're like that round here, though. They know he was poisoned, but they're not interested what with." The shopkeeper looked up at Masters as if willing him to name the poison—perhaps as a quid pro quo after the dissertation on gallipots. But Masters refused to answer the unspoken query. Instead, he said: "Well, I feel pleased to have preserved at least one secret in Limpid. Good-bye, again."

Masters strolled slowly back to the police station and his study of the auction catalogues. He was feeling slightly happier than he had been earlier. Not that he felt he was any nearer the solution of his problem, but the short break and the chat with the tobacconist had done him good. Perhaps it was the feeling of being alone for a time, or maybe the fact that the tobacconist had recognised him had refurbished his vanity. At any rate, he was reluctant to go indoors again. But as he had been about to say to Telford earlier, had he not been interrupted, whenever he was faced with an unpleasant duty his philosophy was to tackle it immediately. So he went up the steps, lifted a hand in reply to the desk sergeant's greeting and made his way to the interview room.

He took off his jacket, opened a window, charged and lit a pipe, and got down to work. Lists! He was interested in some of the items. A few were unknown to him. A clockwork spit? It took him a moment or two to realise that this meant a spit on which to skewer meat, which was then rotated in front of the heat by means of a clockwork motor. An encoignure cupboard? Encoignure? A second or two to appreciate that the word was French and something to do with a corner—a corner cupboard. Commodes seemed to be in good supply. Pie-crust tables. He knew what they were. And a zinc bath with seven assorted pieces of kitchenware. It went on and on. He hadn't any real reason for doing this, but he felt the need to concentrate.

The March catalogue. Lot 129—a decanter and six sherry glasses. Lot 130, two glass bottomed pint tankards. Lot 131....

He sat up with a jerk, remained quite still for a moment and then reached for the invoice books. He found the one for March and turned to the record of sale for lot 131. The name sprang out at him from the counterfoil. The single word—Benson.

He was in a quandary. It was too unexpected. Excitement tingled his flesh, and yet he felt vaguely disappointed. Why had it to be Benson's name there? It didn't mean a rethink of the whole case, because so far he had felt unable to theorise. But now the theories were coming thick and fast. And all of them cast Benson as the villain. That was why Masters was disappointed. He liked Benson. He had agreed with Frimley that Benson should be borne in mind, but that was only lip-service to the idea that no possibilities should be discarded until facts demanded that they should be.

After almost half an hour, he looked at his watch and put the March catalogue and invoice book in his pocket. The other documents he gathered together and carried out to the desk sergeant.

"Lock these up safely somewhere, please."

"Right, sir."

"It's half past five. Will the library still be open?"

"Today it will, sir. Wednesday's half day closing for the shops. The library keeps open to cater for the shop people. Until six, I think it is. I could ring and ask for you, sir."

"Please don't bother. It's just up the street, isn't it?"

"That's right, sir. On the High Street."

"If Mr Green gets in before six, tell him I'm there. If he comes after that, I'll be at the Swan and Cygnets."

"Right, sir."

There were half a dozen people choosing books. Masters spoke to the girl at the counter. When she learned who he was she told him the librarian was in her office, which led off the reference section. Masters found the door and knocked. Inside three minutes, Miss Harrison was herself selecting books for him from the reference shelves. Masters sat at a table and made notes. As he was finishing, Miss Harrison approached.

"We close at six, Superintendent. But if there is a book you would like to borrow overnight. . . ?"

She had been helpful. She was still trying to be helpful. The books she was offering him were reference books and not normally allowed out of the library. He appreciated the gesture and the trust she showed.

"Thank you, Miss Harrison, but I shan't need them." He smiled. "You are so very knowledgeable about your books that you were able to get me everything I wanted immediately. You've been a great help."

"My pleasure."

"It has been very nice meeting you, Miss Harrison. Goodnight, and once again, thank you for your expert co-operation."

As he went out through the double swing doors,

Green was coming up the steps. The Chief Inspector stopped when he saw Masters coming down.

"You got something?"

"Yes. We'll need a session."

"Now?"

"Yes. In the pub. Tell the lads to bring up a tray to my room. We need privacy."

They turned to walk the short distance to the Swan and Cygnets. They progressed in silence. Green seemed to sense that Masters had gone broody—the sign that he was beginning to get to grips with a problem.

There were two chairs. Masters and Reed occupied them, Green sprawled on the bed and Berger perched gingerly on the collapsible case stand.

The beer was in pint tankards. When it had been tasted, Masters began.

"You will remember that this afternoon Mr Telford asked me what the plans for our next move were."

"Bloody sauce!" murmured Green, wiping his mouth with the back of his hand. "He'll want us clocking in next."

"Like you, I felt a bit cross," admitted Masters, "so I spun him a yarn. . . ."

"Conned him, you mean," said Green. "Put him completely in the wrong for the good of his soul."

"That was the idea. But I'd like you to remember that when he asked me personally what I intended to do, I mentioned croton oil and the fact that I felt it must be a museum strain."

"That was a load of baloney, too," asserted Green,

sitting up. "I remember those articles. Nothing about corn seeds in them at all. They were all about naturally occurring mutants in the pre-penicillin age, or just plain resistant strains."

"Fine. So they were. But the phrase or description 'museum strains' had come into my mind, and as I was ad libbing to baffle Telford, they came out. He asked what the hell I meant, so I had to go on a bit to make it sound reasonable."

"So what has happened? You found some croton oil in a museum?"

"Not quite. You remember I was going through the auction brochures to see if I could strike oil? Well, I got to lot 131 in March and woke up with a bit of a jolt. Anybody like to hazard a guess as to what it was?"

Nobody replied. Berger and Reed looked puzzled. Green tried to give the impression he wasn't trying, but his brain was ticking over furiously. As if to prove it, he said: "How about one of those necklaces made from seeds? They used to be made, before plastic came in."

"Good try," replied Masters. "It was an original antique medicine chest."

They stared at him blankly. Then Reed asked: "Do you mean one of those things you hang on the bathroom walls to keep aspirins in and syrup of figs and stuff like that? An old-fashioned one?"

Masters was feeling more than a little dismayed at the dampness of this particular squib, when all of a sudden the blue paper started burning gratifyingly quickly, Berger leapt so violently to his feet that the case stand collapsed.

"Do you mean one of those old travelling medicine chests, Chief? Like the Duke of Wellington carried with him in his carriage in the Peninsula Wars?" The constable had gabbled it out so fast that Masters had to hold up one hand to stop him.

"Quite right. The one in the catalogue is listed as *circa* 1840, so the old boy himself could still have been around when it was made."

Green selected a crumpled Kensitas. "I've heard something about those. They were rather more numerous in this country than overseas because all our nobs used to do the grand tour and tote one along with them. And, of course, the Empire was getting pretty well outflung and people were having to go to all the corners of the earth and so they took their medicine chests with them. Right?"

"Quite right," said Masters. "I went to the public library to find out what I could about them. I made a few notes if you're interested."

"Obviously you expect us to be," retorted Green.

"Don't go on as if you're not bursting to hear," said Masters. "I've known you too long to be taken in with feigned resignation. You're as thirsty for knowledge as you were for that beer when it first came in."

Green grimaced. "If it'll amuse you."

"I'd like to hear," said Reed. "I appear to be the only one who knows nothing about these chests."

Masters consulted his notes. "As you've heard, as people started to travel more and to open up less populated parts of the world, the demand came for apothecaries to start packing medicines for use overseas. Before then, a lot of home-made remedies had been used and up to that time there had been very little provision for jars of pills, potions, ointments and tinctures.

"The chests came into vogue in the late eighteenth century and were produced throughout the nineteenth century. Almost inevitably, as they became known, they were produced in quite large numbers for home use as well as travel."

"What were they made of? Wood?" asked Green.

"According to the books, they were first class examples of the cabinet maker's skill, and were made of mahogany, grained oak, deal, leather and—later—japanned metal. Those in wood combined drawers, trays and cupboards. I saw an illustration of one opened up. It was a heavily made box with a deep hinged lid. The top half of the box was jammed with stoppered bottles, each one labelled with its contents. The bottom half was a drawer which was divided in all manner of ways. Remember the old pencil boxes with sliding lids and sections inside? It reminded me of those. Two sliding lids which met in the middle of the front half. The parts they covered were sub-divided to take plasters, pill boxes, insufflators, safety pins and so on. The two back corners had lift-out tin boxes—perfect cubes with rings in the lids. They were obviously for some very commonly used material—perhaps linseed for poultices in one and salt or lime for cleansing in the other. Between these two was a long space for scissors, forceps, probes, a hank of horsehair, needles for stitching and various other et ceteras I couldn't recognise. Oh, yes! There was a little pestle and mortar, too.

"The book said that the pharmacists who supplied

and stocked the cabinets often included, besides the traditional medicaments, some items made up to the individual customer's requirements."

Masters looked round for comments as he finished. Green, staring up at the ceiling and trying to blow smoke rings, said: "Since croton oil was listed in the British Pharmacopoeia until 1914, and since people in those days were obsessed with having laxatives every day to keep their bowels open—thinking that turning themselves inside out every morning was what made Britain great—you are saying that you think there is a good chance that those medicine chests contained croton oil. Right?"

"Right."

"And since one of these chests has turned up locally, as has a dollop of croton oil which has proved untraceable elsewhere in the country, you are putting two and two together to make your usual five."

"I am asking you to at least consider the chest as not only a possible source of the croton oil, but the probable one."

Green rolled over until he was facing Masters.

"You're right, of course. You've got to be. The coincidence would be too great, else."

"But, sir," said Reed. "Since 1840? Oil over a hundred years old?"

"Have you ever known oil in a stoppered bottle evaporate?" asked Berger. "Or deteriorate? Come on, chum! They even keep port and brandy that long without it going off."

"True enough," replied Masters. "But there was a point made in one of the books I read. It was concerned with dating the chests for the antiquarian's benefit. These chests usually had the original supplier's labels in the lid, set in rows to correspond to the bottles on the top shelf, of which one could only normally see the stoppers and shoulders—as opposed to the labels on the sides. However, the book pointed out that it was as well to remember that the bottles were not always refilled at the pharmacy which originally furnished a chest. So the owner would take along a bottle to be refilled. He wouldn't take the whole chest. A new label would go on the refilled bottle, but the old one would stay in the lid. My point is, that though the chest may be a genuine 1840 model judging by the lid labels, the contents could have been replaced again and again until such time as the chest went out of regular use, and that could be much more recently than 1840."

"Good point," said Green. "So now what we have to do is to establish whether that particular chest actually did contain croton oil. After that the going may be hard or easy. Who knows?" He turned to Masters. "You had the invoice books. Did you look up to see who bought the chest?"

Masters nodded.

"Who?"

After a brief pause, Masters said: "Benson."

There was a moment of shocked silence while this news sank in. Then all three of Masters' listeners tried to speak at once.

"Let's not get too excited," he pleaded. "One at a time. Greeny?"

"All I was about to say was that I am now convinced, without any need to see it for myself, that the cabinet in question *did* contain croton oil, and that the croton oil that killed Hardy came from that cabinet."

"No argument. I felt the same myself. But we shall still have to check."

"And recheck Benson."

"Certainly. Reed?"

"I was going to say, Chief, that even though that chest did contain croton oil and Benson bought it, it doesn't mean to say he ever had the oil."

"I quite agree. You're thinking of the other lot—the glassware—from which the gimmel flask mysteriously disappeared after the sale. You think the croton oil might have walked, too."

"Just a thought, Chief."

"And a very pertinent one. Berger?"

"I was going to say, Chief, that it's one thing to buy a medicine chest which has a bottle of croton oil in it, and quite another to know that the oil is dangerous and can be used for murdering somebody with. Your average chap wouldn't know that. Not one of us had ever heard of croton oil until yesterday, and if none of us knew about it, I don't reckon many others do. So what I'm trying to say is, that we're looking for somebody who knows about medicines and their effects."

"Quite right. Or somebody with enough up top to get to know about them."

"Benson comes in that category," said Green. "He must do a hell of a lot of research and reading to get to know about his antiques and to establish their . . . what's the word. . . ?"

"Provenance."

"Yeah! That's it. He'll always be digging in musty

old books—just the sort of place to find out about croton oil."

"True," said Masters.

"So what's next?"

"Next? What's wrong with a spot of dinner?"

CHAPTER VIII

It was when they were drinking coffee after dinner that Green said: "What about Benson? Can we afford to leave him till tomorrow?"

"I don't intend to. I think we could stroll along there when we're ready and see if he's at home, don't you?"

"Have you told the local boys?"

Masters looked at him pityingly.

"Okay, okay," said Green. "I only asked."

"In that case, the true answer is that when I found the lot in the catalogue and the appropriate invoice, I was alone. None of them were around to tell. That's why I left a message for you and you know where you found me."

The hotel restaurant was barely half full. The term 'early closing' in Limpid seemed to mean that the whole town closed down—a fair indication that the town was, in truth, little more than the shopping centre for the surrounding area. At their table in the corner of the long room they were virtually isolated. If they wished to converse in confidence there seemed to be no reason why they shouldn't.

"I like this pub," said Green. "I like the building and the rooms. The beer's passable . . . if you get my meaning . . . and the grub's not bad. We had that liver pudding at lunchtime and their roast turkey tonight—both good. But I can't understand why they try to con you by cutting a sausage in half and then laying it flat side down on the plate to make it look like a whole one. That's the sort of rotten trick you find all over this country these days. Why, they never did that with NAAFI bangers at the worst period of the war."

"I agree," said Berger. "They want to serve up small ones or cut them out altogether. You can't trust anybody these days."

"Oh, come on," said Reed. "You'd trust a copper, wouldn't you?"

"Not even them," said Green. "Ask the boss."

Reed looked across at Masters. "Don't you trust coppers, Chief?"

"Present company excepted, and a good few others I dare say, there is no reason to suppose that a policeman is any more trustworthy than many other citizens. We in the force are a cross section of the community, in spite of fairly careful selection, and we have the failings of any cross section. By and large, if you're a good copper, you're only good at being a copper. You have a bit more authority thrust on you, of course, and I believe that it is authority which is the downfall of the force. Wrongly exercised authority, I mean, and when I say downfall of the force, I mean on the occasions when it does fall down."

"You reckon it does very often?"

"More often than I like to think. You see, there are some facts that can help police. Take murder as an instance. It is a fact that in over fifty per cent of cases, a near relative of the victim is guilty of his murder. That fact should help us immensely. But unthinking coppers don't use it wisely. They use it, in fact, together with a good modicum of third degree, instead of investigation."

"I don't get you, Chief."

"Then you should. I can quote you at least three cases which have reached the newspapers recently where local detectives have immediately picked up a victim's nearest relative—for no reason other than the fact that he or she was the nearest relative—and subjected them to forms of questioning which are best forgotten. These people, already distressed by the deaths of loved ones, are treated as guilty people, although the slightest attempt at true investigation would have shown them to be innocent. They are invited to confess; told that the police know they have done it; bullied unmercifully; have words put in their mouths. You know the sort of thing: 'Come on and, confess. You went down to the pub, didn't you. You saw her there and didn't like what she was doing. So you clobbered her, didn't you?' The interviewee says no, so then he gets: 'Come on, lad, make it easy for yourself. Confess, and we'll stop.' Or you get the usual one of: 'If you want to play it the hard way, lad, don't blame me?' Or the hard questioner followed by the soft soaper."

"You never use those methods, Chief."

"Never. I consider that they, in themselves, are criminal acts. In the overwhelming environment of a police station you can, by those methods, get anybody to say anything if you go on long enough. If I ever come across it, the officer implicated gets the rough edge of my tongue. But nobody who is being questioned does. If I can't prove a crime and pin it on the villain by my investigatory ability, I don't resort to bullying which will never prove anything."

"You sound bitter, Chief."

"I am. You see I've suffered such treatment."

"You have, Chief?"

"The Detective Chief Inspector here will be able to tell you better than I can. He sorted it out for me."

Reed turned to Green.

"What happened?"

"It's about two years ago now. You've seen your revered boss's private car, have you? It's the sort that catches the eye and rouses a bit of envy now and again. He was tooling along in it at a sedate thirty-five in a forty area one Sunday afternoon. The road was empty and all was serene when a couple of young motor-cycle cops roar up from behind, pull over in front of him and flag him down. He stops like a good citizen and then it starts. Tyres kicked, number plates tugged—the whole treatment. His nibs asks why he has been stopped, and one joker says because the car's been travelling at sixty in a forty area. Now, being the chap he is, the boss does not pull out a warrant card and show it, he merely says that he was doing thirty-five. To his horror, this causes the two boyos to threaten him with a duffing up if he argues with them and he's to remember that it's not only two to one there, on the spot, but it'll be their two words against one in court.

"His confidence in the force thoroughly shaken, his nibs says no more, and when he's asked for his name, just says George Masters—no hint of rank or of being a copper. Then he's let go. Of course, he's out of the

Metropolitan Area where he's known, so those two
don't cotton on to who he is, nor do the people in
their nick, and in due course, the summons comes
through. But his nibs, incensed by what has happened, has already reported the affair at the Yard.
The Yard takes it seriously. It is decided that these
two boyos shall be investigated unbeknown to them.
I'm told off to do it. I don't stop the proceedings, because I'm working behind the scenes. And what I
didn't turn up! It had to be true. Those boyos had
pulled in a capful. Every driver had been alone at the
time. Every car stopped was a class vehicle. And every
one of those drivers swore he had been threatened
with a beating up."

"Then what?"

"All hell was let loose. I got both of them put inside for perverting the course of justice. I got sergeants, inspectors and a Chief Super kicked out,
suspended or demoted, according to their lack of su-
pervision, and I got well over a dozen fines and en-
dorsements squashed. I also made it my business to
have a word or two with the local magistrates about
gullibility and smelling rats when too many cases
from the same cops were too similar, and finally I
gave them the bit about accountability. We had a
clean up there, I can tell you."

Berger was thoughtful. At last he asked: "It's an
eye-opener of a story, but what's the point of it at this
juncture."

"Because we asked," explained Reed.

"Not entirely," said Masters. "What I want you to
understand is that you are public servants and so
have a real duty to the public. I'm not asking you to
be soft with criminals. I couldn't do that, because I'm

too fond of sending them down myself. But a person is innocent until proved guilty. Responsibility sometimes leads to us forgetting that."

"I get it, Chief. There appears to be a lot of evidence against Benson, but you're still going to treat him as a completely innocent man."

"More or less. I shall not haul him off to the nick, I shall not bully him, but I shall question him very closely. I can't guarantee any form of success, but I'll fall over backwards not to harass unduly an innocent man. And believe me, under that gruff exterior which the Chief Inspector sometimes assumes, you will find a kind heart that will not, under any circumstances whatsoever, accept unfairness. He'll put pressure on known criminals. None better. But he knows them and they know him. He's got a philosophy which says that nobody should suffer except those who deserve it."

"So," said Green, "shall we go and see old Benson?"

As Masters got to his feet, Reed asked: "Can we come, Chief?"

Masters nodded. If he was going to weld a team he had to do the field training. He'd taught them how he expected them to behave. Now, perhaps, they might get a glimpse of how reasonable behaviour can pay off even in murder investigations.

"Four of you?" Benson sounded not the least put out by the size of the party. "Come in, all of you. We keep consulting each other, don't we? Shall I go first?"

He limped ahead up the stairs. Reed and Berger coming up slowly in the rear were taking it all in.

Masters heard them whispering about the grill and sensed their admiration for the flat when they eventually reached it. He himself had no definite plan as to how to play his hand. He held a couple of aces. He felt he could afford to let events take their course as long as they kept more or less to the subject in hand. His three companions were all, he felt, completely on his net and should be able to contribute something to the conversation.

Benson saw to it that each had a seat before settling down himself.

"We're a bit of a crowd," explained Masters, "because I believe in trying to keep everyone informed, and Limpid doesn't offer much for young policemen off duty on a Wednesday evening."

"So you brought them along for the ride, to use the modern idiom? Quite right. Would you mind acting as unpaid duty steward, Constable Berger? The drinks are in the wine cupboard. Glasses up top, liquor down below."

Berger got to his feet.

"Ask everybody what they will have. You'll find it all there."

While Berger busied himself, Green said: "We are on the job, Mr Benson. This isn't purely a social call."

"I didn't suppose it was. You have the air of men who are about their business. My only query is, what is the nature of your business? And how can I help? If we could dispose of that, we might find the evening deteriorating into a social chat."

"Deteriorating, sir?"

"In the sense that we might discuss the trivia of life instead of an urgent and distressing problem."

Again Green spoke up. "Distressing?"

"Most assuredly distressing. A community such as this riddled with corruption like a diseased body, and a man murdered. To anybody who is fond of Limpid, the thought of it is distressing."

"You say you are fond of Limpid, sir," said Reed, surprisingly. "Were you fond of Mr Hardy? Was anybody fond of Mr Hardy?"

"I, personally, disliked him intensely, sergeant. So, I imagine did a lot of people. But you must remember that the vast majority probably never came into contact with him."

"Why did you dislike him so much, sir?"

"Now I am going to be completely irrational. I simply didn't like the look of the fellow. At first, that is. We are all guilty of snap judgements. First impressions we call them, and once formed, they take a lot of eradicating. Those judgements are based, particularly on first meeting, on visual impressions, and if the visual impression one receives is unlikeable, then one finds the person unlikeable. Actions—later actions—may, of course, cause one to alter one's opinion, but we are all guilty of prejudice, and even reasonable actions in one whom we dislike may be viewed with a jaundiced eye. We see a good deed as having an ulterior motive; an expression of fine or moral thought as so much hypocritical humbug. The list is endless. And I freely admit to prejudice, except that I call it experience and judgement. I should be a fool if I were not prejudiced against, say, a certain make of motor car that I had found unsatisfactory not just once, but two or three times. And the same goes for people. I form judgements. We all do, if we are to claim any sense of differentiation. So it was with

Hardy. I formed a poor opinion of Hardy and, though it cost me a deal of money, I felt a certain amount of satisfaction when I found my judgement of the man confirmed by his actions."

Reed was still intent on steering the conversation. "What actions were they, sir? Would you care to tell us?"

"By all means, if they are of interest to the others."

"Sir," said Berger, seriously, "it is very important to us to know all we can about the murdered man. I listened to a lecture by Superintendent Masters a few months ago, and he told us that in his experience the actions of the victim or his character caused his death as often as not."

"He didn't say earned or deserved death, I hope?"

"No, sir. Caused. He stressed that point. The murder victim is not always entirely innocent of murder was what he said." The young detectives turned to Masters. "Isn't that right, Chief?"

Masters grimaced. "I'm flattered that my words should have been remembered so well that they can be quoted months later. Your memory has not played you false, young man."

Benson smiled. "I'm very pleased to learn that our police force has such a realised philosophy. And I will certainly gratify the sergeant's request as to why I found Hardy an unlikeable man—by giving one example of his business ethics.

"I have owned this flat now for a few years, but I have known it and liked it all my life. In my young days it was owned by a couple who were older than my own parents, a Mr and Mrs Patch. He was the local registrar, among other things. I think he was the Board School Officer who chased up truants, and he

was clerk to one of the nearby parish councils at an
honorarium of, I believe, twenty pounds a year. It
seems a small sum, these days, but he made all together a good living and he and his wife were happy
here. She, dear soul, taught me at Sunday school
when I was six or seven, and we took a liking for
each other then. Always when I came home, from
school, university or on leave from abroad, I would
visit her, and she would expect it of me.

"The husband died quite a long time ago, but Mrs
Patch continued to live on here alone until about
eight years ago. Then she got the offer of a home
with some niece whom I never met but who was apparently genuinely fond of the old lady. So she decided to sell this flat. She asked Hardy to do it for
her. He put a couple of advertisements in the local
paper and a card in that window of his. He even sent
two or three people to look round in those first few
weeks, but after that, nothing. It was nearly eighteen
months later that I came back to Limpid. I was, by
then, a widower. I was hoping to get somewhere
suitable to live. Naturally, as always, I called on Mrs
Patch. She told me she had tried to sell her flat. Of
course, I was overjoyed. The place wasn't like it is
now, but as I said, I'd always liked it. So I offered to
buy it, there and then. It was a private treaty between
friends. I instructed my lawyer to give Mrs Patch the
price she asked. Hardy did not come into it. But as
soon as he learned of the sale, he demanded his fee.
Mrs Patch had not paid him a deposit—a practice
which I believe is now creeping in with agents—and I
realised Hardy was out of pocket to the tune of a few
pounds, so I went to see him. I thought I would give
him the money to cover his expenses, though I con-

sidered that his business was in the nature of a
gamble. He offers to sell. If he succeeds, he's paid. If
not, he loses a little. But Hardy demanded the full
percentage. I spoke to my lawyer about it. He gave
me as his opinion that because Mrs Patch had not actually withdrawn the flat from Hardy's list, although
Hardy had not actively tried to sell, technically she
was liable for the fee. I didn't want Mrs Patch to suffer, so I settled the account. But Hardy knew my
opinion of him. To treat an elderly widow according
to the strict letter of the law, having made no effort
on her behalf, was in my opinion the action of a
crook. So you see, his subsequent actions reinforced
the opinion I originally formed of him, and that was
that I found him unlikeable. Or as I said at first, I
disliked him."

"Intensely?"

"If I were to qualify it, yes. Intensely. I found him
to be a man who submerged the decencies of life
beneath the exigencies of business—which I saw, in
his case, as the mere making of money for the sake of
making it." Benson looked round. "But I feel I must
be boring you, or preventing you from arriving at the
real purpose of your visit."

"Not in the least—to either point," said Masters
courteously. "As Constable Berger said, we like to
know the background. To get under the skin of a
case."

"Every time?"

"Not every time. Quite often a murder case is no
real problem. Quite a lot of killers make little attempt to hide their crime. They're usually amateurs,
you know. Murder is their first and only crime—the
result of an overwhelming fit of rage, jealousy or

madness of one sort or another. At other times, murder is of the violent type. A criminal's crime. Then
we don't seek atmosphere. We feel our way through
the underworld of villainy, where the answer to everything is a sawn-off shotgun. But here, in Limpid,
which gives you, as you enter it for the first time, a
feeling of serenity and a sense that in such surroundings crime is out of place, out of context, one has to
orientate oneself to deal with the problem. Crime is
unexpected here. One does not anticipate meeting it.
It surprises even people like us who have come here
expressly to solve it. And so we have to adjust to the
atmosphere and the people. It is as though we appeared in a different play each night. Yesterday a
market place in Rome, today the Forest of Arden, tomorrow a castle in Denmark. Different sets, different
words, different plots, different approaches."

"Constable," said Benson, "more beer, if you would
be so kind. I greeted policemen at my door—albeit
men of repute—and I find I am conversing with phi-
losophers. But I feel I should disabuse your minds,
gentlemen. There is a saying round here: 'Farm labourers never open their windows.' And it is a true
saying. They don't. The downstairs windows of labourers' cottages are cluttered with ferns and potted
geraniums and the occupants sleep in their small
stuffy bedrooms without a breath of air."

"Perhaps they get too much fresh air."

"Perhaps. But Limpid is only a gaggle of labourers'
cottages. We never open our windows—figuratively.
We have a serene, picturesque, fresh look outside, but
we have our fair share of foul air inside. There is a
stench in Limpid."

"So we have discovered."

"Are you on the point of opening any windows?"

"We're scratching away at the paint," said Green, accepting a refill from Berger. "But before we can start pushing up the sashes, we need to know a little more. You've done what you might call police work, Mr Benson."

"I've certainly helped to police an area—a slightly different task from the one you are engaged on."

"Still, you'll be aware—from your reading, perhaps—that when there's a murder, it's profitable to look pretty hard at the victim's relatives and close associates."

"I had heard that."

"Hardy had two partners. We've learned this and that about the young one, Lamont, but Williams seems to be unknown. We haven't heard of him. We'd appreciate a word from you about him if that's possible."

"I can give you an impression only, not fact."

"As long as you're not disguising opinion as fact, we shall know how we stand."

Masters sat back. He was quite happy with the way his team was playing this game. He had often resolved crime by listening to gossip. Indeed, the whole informer system which the police relied on so heavily was only a form of culling gossip from a selected few. The grass comes in many guises, from the street-corner tout to the man of culture rare—like Benson. The tout picks up titbits; the Bensons observe and distill opinions. They are both useful when passed on.

"Williams doesn't make the splash that Hardy did. Nor is he so brash as Lamont. A more subtle man, I would say. He is the sort of man who has succeeded in his calling by academic ability, whereas Hardy has been a lucky opportunist and a blusterer. Hardy has needed the trappings—his seat on the council, his large house and so on—to prove to himself that he has succeeded. Williams, I believe to be a man who can assess himself more rationally."

"You mean his bank balance is enough indication of success. He doesn't have to splurge to prove it?"

"That could be one way of putting it. We hear a lot these days of the two cultures—the sciences and the humanities. I deplore the division, because so much human endeavour must fall outside of both. I believe the house agent to be an example of this. Can one really drop such a man into either category? Some may argue that it is possible, but whereas I tend to class Hardy and Lamont with the rather more deplorable class of second-hand car salesman, I view Williams as an entirely different creature. I would not call him a cultured man, exactly, but semi-cultured perhaps."

"I've got it, sir," said Berger. "If we think of people as pearls, there are the genuine ones at the top end, the paste ones at the bottom end, and the cultured pearls in the middle. Williams is a cultured one."

Benson laughed, Masters smiled, and Green said: "By the lord Harry, we've got a thingumitite with us . . . a sort of visionary. Young cops with fantouche ideas!"

Berger reddened. "Sorry, sir. It just came into my mind."

"Don't be sorry," said Benson. "If that's the pattern you've built from my words, so be it."

Masters said: "Would it surprise you to know that Williams is a crook?"

"Not in the least. But if true, I'd say he wouldn't be a crude crook like Hardy. I've used the word subtle in describing him."

"Accurately, I think, sir. This afternoon you advised me to consult the companies' register. I had that done. The Goodwerry set-up has two directors, one of whom is Yorkwall, the other Williams."

"Williams? Not Hardy?"

"Williams."

"I'm surprised."

Benson frowned in concentration for a few moments. Masters watched him carefully: saw the puzzlement begin to disappear, and when the older man looked up, asked: "Subtle, Mr Benson?"

"If my interpretation is correct, yes, very subtle. Do you think he conceived the plan? To leave out the H.W.L. offices in order to leave Hardy free to protest so strongly that the plan was, apparently, defeated by fair democratic means?"

"Has it his touch?"

"It certainly hasn't Yorkwall's."

"Would he then have made sure Hardy protested vigorously? Put pressure on him of the 'if you don't do something about it we'll be next' variety?"

"Why not? If he could conceive the original plan, he could certainly contrive to encourage Hardy to act. After all, not only would Hardy lose financially were his office to go, but here was a chance for him to appear as the defender of the oppressed."

"Quite. Has it also occurred to you, Mr Benson, that by collecting three thousand signatures protesting against the bogus proposals you were aiding and abetting Williams in his deception?"

"It has. But I plead the best of intentions."

"I don't doubt that for a moment. But you have spoken of foul air in Limpid. How long have you known it to be here?"

Benson was not quite as ready to answer. When he did, it was not a direct reply.

"What you are asking, Superintendent, was whether I ought not to have suspected or even anticipated some such illegal move before I acted in defence of Theraby."

"You must agree you could not have arrived at all your conclusions concerning goings-on in Limpid since Hardy died on Sunday."

"True. I believe I have known all was not well for a considerable time. But I suppose I have been too idle to expose what I honestly thought of as sharp practice rather than illegal practice. Hardy's death was the penny that dropped. It brought the slot machine into focus and I was able to see for the first time the full import of what had been going on. I honestly believe that is the true answer."

"In that case I will accept it unreservedly."

"I appreciate your assurance."

"Now that's all fine and dandy," said Green, "but what about this character Lamont? I've heard about his wife and his extravagances. I've even met him in the flesh. I'd say he was a one-time whizz kid gone to seed, but I'd like to know his background."

"As to that," said Benson, "the answer is short. He came into the auctioneering and surveying world at a rather late age. He was well into his twenties when he joined Hardy and Williams. His parents put him in there after he had failed at a number of things. I think he realised it was his last chance. Not that he is without intelligence. It is simply that he does not use it to the best advantage."

"What had he done before he joined Hardy and Williams?"

"I wasn't resident in Limpid then, but I understand he tried his hand at starting up a potato crisp factory, growing mushrooms, and clerking with the Electricity Board. There were probably other ventures. In fact I'm almost sure there were. His parents rescued him each time, until they had had enough."

"You told me he had approached you about antiques from time to time."

"He has, and I formed the opinion then that he was a fairly intelligent fellow, capable of learning, but incapable of adopting the right approach to what he set out to achieve. He wanted to learn about antiques in order to make money. I believe he realised that he was in a unique position to find valuable pieces if only he knew how to recognise them. He also believed, I feel sure, that he could sell them without anybody being the wiser, without paying tax as a regular dealer would be required to do. No doubt he would have got away with it if he had adopted an intellectual approach. To be a man who knows about antiques—as with all other subjects—one must study the items, research them, learn to recognise differences, similarities and, by and large, to regard the pieces as a serious adjunct to life. Somebody once said that a collector must be a perceptive person attuned to the aura of the past and interested in adding a new dimension to his present. And it is only within this frame of knowledge and confidence that a collector can hope to know what is good and what is not. Antiques—in a true collector's view—

should be loved and admired and not considered solely as merchandise. Lamont, I fear, had no time to learn how to recognise what was good and what was not; he merely wanted to know which pieces to buy in order to resell at a profit."

"A right philistine, in fact," said Green.

"As you say." Benson pushed himself up out of his chair. "Perhaps I could show you one or two of my prizes."

"Yes, please," said Masters, "but just before you do so, Mr Benson, could I ask you one more question."

"Please do."

"How does rumour in Limpid say Hardy died?"

"Everyone knows that he was poisoned."

"But there are scores of poisons. Which one does Limpid say was used?"

"Ah! Now you have caught me out, Mr Masters. I have heard a number of substances mentioned. Theraby, for instance, says that as he died so quickly he must have ingested strychnine, while others tell more or less horrific tales of insecticides having got into the food. But as yet, to my knowledge, opinion in Limpid has not settled on the culprit."

"And what in your view was the substance used?"

"I just don't know. Don't tell me *you* haven't discovered which substance was used?"

"The pathologists discovered that information for us very quickly."

"What was it?"

"Do you mind if I don't tell you?"

"Of course not. Your professional secrets are yours to keep until you wish to divulge them. But your answer has intrigued me more than ever. The poison itself has become an enigma. I shall have to think

about it—to see if I can't come up with a reason for
your reticence."

Masters laughed and got to his feet. "I'm not proposing to hold out on you too long, Mr Benson."

"You are hoping then to surprise me?"

"If I were to say yes to that, it would be the literal
truth. But I should be disguising the fact that I
should be hoping to surprise something *out* of you."

"Something you feel I have been concealing from
you."

"I hope so."

"I don't understand."

"I don't mean to imply that you have been
concealing it from me knowingly, but I hope you will
be able to help me."

"Please ask whatever it is you want to know."

"Very well. I should like to see the medicine chest
you bought at auction in March."

"The medicine chest? Of course. Only too pleased.
It's over. . . ." Benson stopped in mid-sentence,
and halted his slow walk across the room. He looked
round at Masters. "I was about to tell you it is complete, filled with stoppered glass bottles, many of
which still contain the original medicaments."

"I thought it must be."

"Why?"

"Those are surely the most sought-after specimens.
A complete chest would be a great find. I can't imagine you going for anything less than a good specimen
of any item."

"Mr Masters, you were honest enough to say you
were hoping to surprise something *out* of me, and
then you asked to see my chest, having behaved

rather mysteriously about the poison that killed Hardy. Am I right in believing that you hope to find that poison in the chest in this room?"

"I am."

"Am I to understand from that reply that you suspect me of murdering Hardy?"

"No."

"No? When you expect to find the poison in my possession?"

"No. If that astounds you, Mr Benson, I will again ask you if you know what poison was used?"

"I have no idea."

"Excellent. But if you still feel uneasy at not being under suspicion, I will set your mind at rest by using the old bromide. Everybody is under suspicion until the murderer has been found."

Benson shook his head. "I can't say I'm not relieved at your words, but you're not at all what I imagined a senior detective to be."

Green said: "We like to be different, Mr Benson. What about a gizz into this chest of yours while we still remember?"

"Of course. It is the mahogany box on the top of the bookcase on the far wall. Perhaps one of you would carry it over."

"Leave it to me, sir," said Reed, and hurried across to fetch it. Whilst he was doing so, Benson said: "I have examined the contents and even looked some of them up. I wouldn't have said there was a deadly poison there. There are things like nutmeg, which apparently was used as a tonic. Zinc ointment, which was still in use in my day. As indeed was tincture of rhubarb and sweet nitre. There's flowers of sulphur, powdered lime, linseed for poultices and various samples made from flowers. Oh, I was forgetting!"

"What?"

"A stomach mixture with deadly nightshade in it."

Masters shook his head.

"No?"

Benson remained quiet as the box was put on the table in the centre of the room. A big, ornate brass keyhole plate, three inches by two, graced the front of the box, but there was no key. When Masters remarked on it, Benson told him that he was having one made by hand. A locksmith who specialised in such things had brought soft steel blinds down from London and had filed out the prototype here in this room. The brass one would be cast from the mould and should be ready soon.

Benson lifted the lid. On the inside of it were still eighteen original labels, stained, browned at the edges and coming unstuck at the corners. Standing proud from the tray, just far enough for ease of lifting, were sixteen glass-stoppered bottles, not laid out in the three rows of six that the labels would have led one to expect, but filling the space nonetheless, smaller bottles across the front—seven of them—the remainder anyhow. Masters peered at the labels in the lid. They were almost illegible, but he recognised the shortened form of some words of medical dog-latin—pulv., alb., mist. With care he began to lift out some of the bottles, starting with the front row. The third one he held up to get the light on the label caused a little sigh of satisfaction to escape from his lips.

"That one?" asked Benson.

"Oil of *Croton Tiglium*."

"That?" queried Benson. "That's not a poison, it's jollop. The medical dictionary says it's a cathartic widely used in the last century."

"If it really was widely used," said Green, "no wonder so many of our Empire builders died of dysentery, and people complained of long service in bad stations."

Benson rubbed his eyes with his hand. "Will somebody please explain to me how a laxative made in the nineteenth century could be used for murder in the twentieth century?"

"Sit down, Mr Benson," said Masters in a kindly voice. Only when their host had done so did the Superintendent explain how violent a cathartic croton oil was, how it blistered and burned flesh like mustard gas and how even medical students were warned against testing it.

"Why ever was it put in a medicine chest?"

"I suppose it was diluted to reduce its potential. Two drops in a tumbler of water, perhaps. I honestly don't know, but it was removed from the British Pharmacopoeia in 1914 because of its dangerous nature."

"I reckon they carried it for their horses," said Green. "Mixed a teaspoonful in a bran mash for a constipated horse and it saw it all right for a year."

Masters ignored this observation and continued to talk to Benson. "So you see, sir, if Hardy took upwards of half a tablespoonful of croton oil, thinking it to be salad oil, the results would have been quickly fatal. I can't believe that adding vinegar to fill the spoon and to mix with the oil would neutralise its action in any way. In any case, however much he took, it killed Hardy."

"And you believe that the oil came from that bottle?"

"I do, sir. There is still half an inch left in the bottom, so we know there was a supply here. I can also tell you that every drug house, drug wholesaler, retail chemist and hospital chemist in the country has been asked if they have croton oil in their stocks. None has. It seemed there was no source in this country from which it could have come—until I read that there was this old medicine chest in Limpid, in your possession. Do you think I was wrong to be so sure the oil came from this bottle?"

"Of course not. Your reasoning was sound, your logic impeccable. It would be stretching coincidence too far to suppose otherwise."

"That's what I thought. The only other possibility would have been a supply which came from abroad. But that would argue a degree of pre-planning which I somehow cannot connect with this murder. It was carefully carried out, of course, but in an ad hoc way. What I mean by that is, that if you can plan a murder so thoroughly that you go to lengths of importing the means, you do not bring in croton oil. You bring in something more traditional which you can use without waiting for your victim to have a salad for lunch and which doesn't depend upon exchanging and stealing gimmel flasks. My belief is that croton oil was used simply because it was here to be used."

"But," protested a bewildered Benson, "that would argue a murderer with a knowledge of medicine or at least of the properties of croton oil."

"True." Masters didn't dwell on this point. Instead

he started a new tack. "So you see, Mr Benson, I shall have to ask you for a list of everybody who has been in your flat since you brought the chest two months ago. Particularly anybody who has had any dealings with the chest, or who has been left alone with it in this room at any time while you have made coffee, say, or gone to the lavatory."

Benson nodded.

"To begin with," said Masters, "there is the locksmith you talked of. He must have had the chest open for a very long time, both in and out of your presence. And your housekeeper—Mrs Taylor—isn't it? She'll have been here alone many times in the last two months."

"No! Not Mrs Taylor. It's unthinkable that she should . . . no! It's unthinkable. As unthinkable as. . . ."

"As what, Mr Benson? Or should I say who? Who else whom you consider to be incapable of crime have you had here in connection with the box?"

Benson now looked throughly miserable. "Jack and Jill Racine," he said quietly. "They came to photograph it. They've recently photographed all my items. But I wanted special shots of this one to illustrate an article I was proposing to write on it. They were here some time, but they're young, nice, harmless people. Hard working kids who wouldn't hurt anybody."

"We're very anxious not to incriminate innocent people, Mr Benson. But somebody gave Hardy a dose of croton oil from this bottle. Let us assume that it wasn't you. So who was it? It seems pretty certain it must have been a visitor to your flat."

"Mrs Horbium," murmured Benson. "She asked to

see the chest after she knew I'd bought it. She came with Joanna Wellerby."

"And you left them in here while you went to make them tea or coffee, like a good host does?"

"Yes."

"There'll be others come to mind if you think about it. Why not sleep on it and prepare me a list tomorrow morning?"

"I shall do that, of course, even though I'm hoping against hope you are wrong."

Green said: "Cheer up, Mr Benson. If we *are* wrong, you'll know a lot sooner once we get the list and can check it out."

"In that case, I shall start the list now. No, I don't wish you to go, gentlemen. If for no other reason, you must stay to take the names I give you. Constable, there is still a little something in the wine cupboard or, alternatively, there is coffee in the kitchen—and biscuits if anybody would like a snack. How about rummaging while I set to work here?"

Berger and Reed went to the kitchen after Masters said he would welcome a cup of black coffee. While Benson wrote, Masters and Green chatted in low voices.

"We'll have to take that bottle, George. Do you want the whole chest?"

"Just the bottle, I think. No need to deprive the old boy of his treasure. But it makes me sweat to think of the lethal substances there must be littered across the countryside. Don't forget that the bottle here is not necessarily the only consignment of that particular poison in Limpid."

"How d'you mean?"

"If the gimmel flask is still in existence it may still have some in it."

"Oh, that! For one moment I thought you were going to come up with a bright idea about some other source of this croton muck." Masters grimaced. Green went on: "Old Telford isn't going to be too pleased when he knows the stuff he scoured the country for was sitting not four hundred yards from his own nick."

"What he'll be most annoyed about is that we found it, and found it without his two men being present. I've a feeling he's going to accuse me of not sticking to the spirit of our agreement to take them on the strength."

"You're worried about that, I'll bet. Hell's bells, somebody had to find it."

"Local pride is fierce. We don't always appreciate that when we are called in the locals not only resent us taking over a job they feel they can't do, but they're also a bit touchy that such crime as we are called on to investigate lets down the whole of a tight little community such as this one in Limpid. We hurt both civic and professional pride."

"Well hard luck! Ah, Mr Benson! Finished, is it, sir?"

"Complete to the best of my knowledge. If I think of any additions I will contrive to give them to you tomorrow."

Masters took the list. There were 23 visits on it. None of the names, other than those mentioned to him previously, were familiar to him.

"Now for the coffee," said Benson. "Oh, by the way, did you notice, when you looked into the chest, the little scales, the ointment slab and the plaster iron? No? Come along, I'll show you them."

"He's back on top," whispered Green to Masters as they got to their feet.

CHAPTER IX

Masters lay awake when he got to bed. He had again read the list supplied by Benson, and though he accepted that any of the people whose names appeared on it could have been guilty of murdering Hardy, he felt inclined to disregard those that were unfamiliar to him. He intended to have them checked out, of course, but more as a matter of form than out of any hope that he would find corn in Egypt by so doing.

So far, though they had no firm suspect, Green was inclined to favour Lamont as the man to look at. He had a knowledge of gimmel flasks. He had tried to buy one at an auction. He was said to be in financial straits through enforced high living. He was to be seen around with Joanna Wellerby. He—according to Benson—might be getting less than his fair share of Hardy's dealings with the ring. He was somebody who could come and go in the Hardy garden at any time without remark. He would know Hardy's liking for an oil and vinegar dressing, that Hardy was on a salad diet, that he used a gimmel flask at table. And Lamont, as a fully fledged partner, would almost certainly stand to gain financially by Hardy's death. All circumstantial evidence that would lead one to suspect Lamont, but the big gap in the case against him was that he had not visited Benson since the medicine chest had been in the latter's flat, and it was certain that nobody could have broken in there unbeknown to Benson. Of course, Lamont could have tried to acquire the croton oil through a second person—an agent—like Joanna Wellerby, perhaps? Masters thought not. Joanna Wellerby might be so fond of male company that she was not too particular as to its quality, but he was convinced she would draw the line at actively aiding and abetting murder. She might make use of Lamont because there was no better male available, but she must have a knowledge of his true worth. He was just not worth risking her liberty and an outstanding musical career for—always assuming she was willing to connive at murder in the first place, which Masters doubted.

So where could Lamont have got the croton oil from if she had not tried to get it? Tried? Something clicked in Masters' brain. He got out of bed and took the invoice book from his jacket pocket. Benson had paid . . . he turned the leaves . . . he remembered noticing that Benson had paid . . . yes! There it was. Benson had paid twenty-one pounds for the chest. That must mean he bought it against opposition. Benson would be too wily a buyer to make an opening bid of twenty-one pounds. Besides, the amount was not the opening bid an auctioneer would call for. Twenty, perhaps, or twenty-five, but not twenty-one. So somebody had forced Benson up. Somebody besides Benson had wanted the medicine chest. Not an ordinary buyer's item. No housewife would want an old box of bottles. The ring then?

Masters thought not. If the ring had wanted it, the price would be more than twenty-one pounds before they dropped out. So who? Masters looked at his watch. Twenty past twelve. Benson would be in bed. Masters gave up the idea of calling him.

As soon as he had breakfasted next morning he got to his feet.

"Where away?" asked Green, spreading marmalade an inch thick on toast. "Forgotten something?"

"I'll be down again in two minutes, then I'm going along the street to see Benson. If you're ready when I get down, you can come with me."

"Thanks." Green bit into the toast with a noise like a coke-hammer breaking into action. Then he spoke through the mouthful. "I recognise the signs. You got an idea after you went to bed last night." He used a finger to take a blob of marmalade from the corner of his mouth. "And I know from experience that whatever it was is going to be significant. I'll be at the door, waiting."

A minute or two later, as they walked the hundred and fifty yards to Benson's flat, Masters said: "I'll not try to tell you about it. It'll appear as we talk with Benson." Green grunted his assent to this arrangement, and no more was said until they came to the flat door between its flanking shops, which were now beginning to open.

The door was opened by a woman Masters had not seen before, but it did not need much acumen to guess who she was.

"Mrs Taylor? My name is Masters. Could I have a word with Mr Benson, please?"

"Well, he's just having his breakfast."

"I'm sure he won't mind our seeing him. We are

policemen, you know." This worked the oracle. Once more they climbed the stairs into the flat.

"I thought I heard your voices," said Benson. "Two more cups, Mrs Taylor, please."

"No, thank you, Mr Benson. There is just one quick question I would like to ask you and it's this. Who was bidding against you at the auction for the medicine chest?"

"Only one person."

"I guessed as much. Somebody who withdrew at twenty pounds?"

"Quite right. Bert, the head porter, was against me."

"Bert Spooner?" asked Green incredulously. "He went to twenty pounds for . . . for that?"

Benson laughed and offered Green a cigarette. "Not on his own behalf, Mr Green."

"Whose then?"

"For the man on the stand at the time, I think."

"Who was that?"

"Lamont."

Masters and Green exchanged glances. "You think? Can you be sure?"

"Not absolutely, but the way the bidding was conducted led me to believe so at the time. I can see no reason for not still thinking so."

"Can you tell me what went on?"

"In detail." Benson then proceeded to recount how Lamont had not called for an opening bid, but had announced that he already had one for four pounds. Then Benson went through the bidding, much as a top bridge player can remember months later how a certain hand has been played.

"Thank you," said Masters when the account was finished.

"Wait a moment," said Benson. "The importance of your question has not escaped me. But I would ask you to remember that I can see no way that Lamont could have taken the croton oil from the chest while it has been in my possession, and if he had extracted some of it earlier, why then he wouldn't have needed to buy the chest."

"The point.has not escaped me, Mr Benson. Now we'll leave you to finish your breakfast."

"He's right, you know," said Green when they were once more in the street.

"Of course he is. I knew that before we came. If Lamont had really wanted that chest for the croton oil it contained, he would not have dropped out at twenty pounds. But if he had wanted it for the sake of making money, then he would have known that to go too high would mean that all chances of making profit would disappear. So he had to put a limit beyond which he could not go. He told Bert to go to twenty and not a penny more."

"So we're eliminating Lamont?"

"We're eliminating him. But we've got to see him just as soon as possible."

Masters finished telling his assembled team about locating the croton oil.

"Quite honestly," said Wally Frimley, "I don't know how you lot manage it."

"Neither do we," replied Green, "and if we did we wouldn't be able to tell you."

"So what's the form?" asked Hoame. "We looked for the croton oil and couldn't find it. You looked for the gimmel flask and couldn't find it, but you did find the oil. What do we look for now in the hope of finding something different?"

"Sir," said Berger solemnly, looking at Hoame, "you're off net. We at the Yard . . ." he glanced across at Green to see how he would take this claim from an understrapper who had not yet been forty-eight hours in this particular team, ". . . we at the Yard, never look for just one thing at a time, particularly in the early stages of an inquiry. We may state a pin-point objective, but we advance on a broad front: a sweep which gathers in everything in its path. One has to be prepared to do that. Look at the information that has been netted while we have been making enquiries about gimmel flasks. And to be fair to yourself, we even got on the track of that while you were present."

Hoame stared at the constable. He could hardly deny what had been said, but he didn't look as if he much cared for even such obvious truths being pointed out to him by a junior officer. Green, however, appeared to like it. "Couldn't have put it better myself," he said. "Never close your mind to possibilities or opportunities, Colin."

Hoame nodded. "So what will be our pin-point objective today?"

Masters stepped in. "You've got the names of the people who have called on Benson since he bought the chest. I want them checked out, to see if they interest us. The way I would like it done is to find out if they have alibis for between twelve and two last Sunday. If they have, they're out of the reckoning for obvious reasons. If they haven't, I want to know something about them which, so far, we have not paid any attention to. It is this. For somebody to use croton oil as a poison would argue some knowledge of the medical, pharmaceutical or biological sciences in general. Try to find out—indirectly if needs be—whether any of these people who have no alibis for Sunday lunchtime have such a knowledge."

"Are you in on this, George?" asked Frimley.

"Not until a little later. Greeny and I have had a call from the Yard. . . ."

"You're not going back, I hope?"

"No. But there's something we must see to. It will take an hour at least. That may not be too bad a thing as it turns out. You and Colin are locals, and you'll be able to deal with Benson's visitors more quickly than we could. So if you, Wally, will take Reed and my car, while Colin takes Berger in his car, you may be able to break the back of it by the time we're ready to join you. Divide the list up how you like, Wally, and ring in here, both of you, at eleven, to see if we're ready to join you."

"Right." Frimley sounded pleased to be given a job to do on his own. "We'll get off straight away."

"Okay," said Green when they were alone, "you didn't get a call from the Yard. You wanted to get rid of that lot."

"Yes, I did," said Masters petulantly. "I can't work with them tied to my tail. I can't think, either, with them wanting to know every tick my brain makes and why. In the old days, we seemed to sense what each other was about and accepted that whatever any other member of the team was doing was part of an overall plan of investigation that never had to be spelled out once it was on the move."

"So you want to think. Where do I come in?"

"I've been thinking, or trying to, along lines suggested by something you said last night."

"What, for instance?"

"As near as I can remember them, your words were: I thought you were going to come up with some bright idea about some other source of this croton muck? Remember?"

"I remember. But I wasn't saying there *was* another source. I was saying I hoped to hell there wasn't."

"I can't argue with you, but earlier you had made some remark about the possibility of there being two gimmel flasks. Now you may say that both remarks were just unconnected comments on the chit-chat that was going on at the time they were made, but they could just be an indication that you were toying with the idea—subliminally, perhaps—that certain aspects of this case might be duplicated."

"You reckon? If I was, I need my head examined."

"All right, examine it. Or rather the facts stored away in it, and tell me what you come up with."

Green scowled, took out a new packet of Kensitas and broke it open without saying a word. Masters strolled to the window and stood looking out over the station yard as he charged his pipe. The silence reigned for two or three minutes before Green growled: "This isn't fair, George. You've sown an idea, and I can't get it out of my mind so's to make an unbiased assessment. And there's something missing. It's incomplete. What I mean is, I can think up several things, or I would be able to if . . . no, its like trying to make something without several parts, one of which is vital if the structure is to stand up."

"What part?"

"That's the trouble. I don't damned well know, do

I? If I did I might be able to do something about it."
Green glowered and crushed out his cigarette. "It's
like trying to build a boat without having a keel to
lay down. You can't begin. But if it was only the mast
missing, well you could get a hell of a long way before you had to go looking for a pole."

Masters sat down opposite him. "Would this help?"
He took the March sale catalogue out of his inside
pocket and put it on the table so that Green could
read its cover.

"This? How could this help, unless . . . hey,
don't tell me there were two medicine chests for sale
that day and you stopped looking after you discovered what you did about the first one?"

"No. Try again."

Green contemplated the catalogue which by now
was becoming a bit dog-eared. He read the cover. He
flicked through the pages. "Two!" he muttered. "You
said I'd put the idea of two into your head, and
you've found two of something here. What? Okay, I'll
buy it. I suppose it's staring me in the face and I
can't see it."

"On the cover," said Masters. "Hardy, Williams
and Lamont, Estate Agents and Surveyors. Valuations
carried out. Property handled, et cetera, et cetera, 17
Market Hill, Limpid and. . . ."

"Three, High Street, Coleford" whooped Green.
"Two addresses." He suddenly sobered and looked
across at Masters. "This was why you said you were
going to see Lamont."

"It opens up possibilities, doesn't it?"

Green selected another cigarette. As he lit it he
asked: "When do we go? Now?"

*   *   *

Lamont was in his office and alone when Masters and Green were shown in.

"I understand from our chief clerk that you took certain documents from this office without giving a receipt," he said, clearly under the impression that attack was the best form of defence on this occasion.

"Rubbish," said Green. "They were given to Constable Berger by your staff. And what's more, we're keeping them. If you want to stand on principle, I'll have the Chief Constable send you an official receipt. But as they're stuff you've finished with—or should have—as they all referred to the last fiscal year, what's your interest in them?"

"They're needed for tax purposes."

"Rubbish again. You don't list every single item sold in your returns. They go into the book as a total for the day. And don't try to tell me your Chief Clerk hasn't got the totals. So I'll ask again. What's your great personal interest in those invoice books?"

"None. They are part of the firm's documents."

Masters pulled a chair up and sat down. "You know they'll be safe with us. If the Inland Revenue has any queries concerning them, you can always refer them to the police Documents Squad."

"Who the hell are they?"

"They're a part of what you would refer to as the fraud squad."

Lamont looked sullen. "What do they want them for? There's no fraud there. They're quite straightforward."

"In which case, Mr Lamont, you have no worries. Either you or Mr Williams."

"I haven't."

"Excellent. But you must appreciate that when the

senior partner of a company such as this is suddenly
poisoned for no apparent reason, his business transac-
tions must be investigated in case the motive for murder is to be found there."

"It won't be."

"Oh?" said Green. "You know the motive, do you,
Mr Lamont?"

"Of course not."

"Then why be so adamant about the motive not
being caused by business? You favour social causes, do
you?"

"How the hell do I know?"

"You are his partner."

"What's that supposed to mean?"

"That you ought to be able to make as reasoned a
guess as anybody as to why he was murdered."

"Well, I can't."

Masters started to fill his pipe. "You don't mind if I
smoke, Mr Lamont? Thank you. Now, I'd be interested to know what you and Mr Williams have decided to do about the business."

"How do you mean?"

"Surely my meaning is obvious." Masters struck a
match and held it to his pipe. "There are now only
two of you instead of three. Are you proposing to introduce another partner—senior or junior? Or are you
simply going to concentrate your work here in Limpid, and let the Coleford office go?"

"Nothing's definite yet. Mrs Hardy will have to be
consulted, for one thing."

"Surely not! She'll be a considerable shareholder,
no doubt, but not an active business partner. You and
Mr Williams must have the say in the day-to-day run-

ning of affairs. So tell me, what are the proposals you
will put to Mrs Hardy?"

"It's no secret, is it chum?" asked Green.

Lamont shrugged. "Hardy ran this office. Williams
ran the Coleford office. But as this is the bigger place,
I came in to help Hardy."

"Williams didn't need an assistant?"

"Not a partner. He's got a male clerk and a couple
of typists there. Often enough, Williams only needed
to be over there in the mornings. He was here in the
afternoons."

"That sounds an admirable arrangement," said
Masters. "But what now?"

"I'm going to take over Williams' work at Coleford
while he comes and takes over here full time. I'll be
here, too, in the afternoons."

"Any more partners?"

"No. Our chief clerk here is to be given a rise in
salary to take over more responsibility, and we're getting another clerk in to do some of his work."

"Sounds eminently satisfactory," murmured Masters. "Now tell me, Mr Lamont, does your Coleford
subsidiary conduct auctions as you do here in Limpid?"

"Yes. Not as often and not as big, usually. It's quite
a simple arrangement, really. Limpid will only stand
one big sale a month. So, if there's more than enough
for here, we have an auction in Coleford about every
two months. We hold Coleford items for sale in Coleford if this happens. There's no point in transporting
them all here if they can be sold there."

"Saves a few ackers, I suppose," said Green. "I'd
like to see the Coleford catalogues for a few months
back."

"Why? They're exactly the same as those we have here."

"Nevertheless," said Green, "I'm interested. I suppose I can get them in the back office from Mr Williams' typist, can't I?"

Before Lamont could protest at this action, Green had left the office. Masters, relaxed, asked: "Do you know how Mr Hardy died?"

"Of course I do. He was poisoned."

"How?"

"He was given something in his lunch, wasn't he?"

"Yes, he was. But what was he given?"

Lamont frowned. "I haven't a clue. When I saw Mrs Hardy, she said she thought it must have been the salad dressing, because the police wanted the bottle and it had gone. But they didn't know at first what the poison was, and if they found out later, they didn't tell her."

"I see. Did you know what salad dressing Mr Hardy used?"

"Of course. Oil and vinegar. Out of one of those twin bottles."

"Don't you mean a gimmel flask, Mr Lamont?"

Lamont reddened. "Yes I do. But I didn't think you'd know."

"Obviously."

"Now what are you getting at?"

"The term gimmel flask is not widely known, is it, Mr Lamont?"

"Not really, I suppose."

"So little known, in fact, that even a collector like Mrs Horbium had not heard of it until a week or two ago when you mentioned it in her presence, and that of Mrs Wellerby."

"What's this got to do with Hardy's death?"

"Quite a lot, Mr Lamont. Tell me, when you got Bert Spooner to bid for those twenty-seven pieces of assorted glassware for you, why did you then give the lot back immediately to Bert?"

Lamont glowered. "Because what I thought was there, wasn't."

"Thought, Mr Lamont? Or knew?"

"What do you mean?"

"Mr Lamont, gimmel flasks aren't considerable antiques, but they're liked quite a lot."

"So?"

"So when the gimmel flask you wanted had gone from among that glassware, you gave the rest away."

Lamont nodded.

"Now look, Mr Lamont. You knew that flask was in that lot, because you had made the lots up, hadn't you? But why didn't you just steal it then, if you'd wanted it? It was most unlikely that anybody would miss it."

Lamont didn't reply.

"Or would somebody have missed it? Somebody who knew it was there and who might have remarked on its absence? Come on, Mr Lamont? Who?"

"If you must know, Williams was with me when we estimated the lots. He did that sort of thing. If he thought the day would not bring in enough he added or substituted a few better pieces."

"Or if he thought there were too many good items for the market to stand, he withdrew a few for a later sale, in order to keep prices up?"

"It's the usual practice. There's nothing against the law in it."

"Nothing at all. But Williams was interested in the gimmel flask?"

"Yes. He said he'd like it, just to be upsides with Hardy, and he's a bit of a stickler. If I'd lifted it then, he'd have known. So I thought I'd bid for it."

"Having taken care to hide it in a job lot of twenty-seven pieces of assorted glassware in the hope that nobody would notice its presence and you'd get the lot for a couple of bob?"

Lamont shrugged.

"Was it Mr Williams who told you it was called a gimmel flask and suggested it might be worth a few pounds?"

"He told me it was a gimmel flask, but I didn't know its value—only that it might be worth something as he was so keen to have it."

"I see. So you bought the lot, through Bert, because you were on the stand at the time. But when you came to collect it at the end, the flask was missing?"

"That's right."

"Any idea who could have taken it?"

"It could have been anybody in that mob. Once the selling stops, the Corn Exchange becomes like the Albert Hall at the Proms."

"Where was Mr Williams at the time?"

"Oh, he'd been on the rostrum before me and had gone to lunch."

"You're certain of that?"

"Of course I am. If he'd been in the Exchange, he'd have put in a bid for that flask. He didn't—so he wasn't there. Otherwise I wouldn't have got it for what I paid."

"Quite. But he returned to the sale later—before it ended?"

"Of course. He always checked the chief clerk's figures, and it's done on the spot. It has to be. So many things are verbal that you'd forget half of them if you waited till next morning. Besides there's a hell of a lot of cash to be counted, bagged, and deposited in the bank night safe."

"I see."

"But if you're thinking Williams would take that flask, you're mistaken. I told you he is a stickler."

"For honesty, square dealing, and that sort of thing?"

"Yes. As if any estate would miss the price of that flask!"

"Ah! But if the flask could go, why not other items? Perhaps big, valuable ones?"

"Nobody would do anything like that."

"No? How much do you know about the operations of Bert Spooner and his brother Bandy?"

"Well . . . not much, but I've never found them nicking things."

"Let me give you a tip for the future, Mr Lamont. Those men handle pieces of furniture. They also sell secondhand, seasoned wood. Now that wood comes from. . . ."

"Broken furniture," said Lamont. "Stuff we can't sell."

"But how does it come to be broken, Mr Lamont? You see it after it arrives at your warehouse. I think quite a lot of it is broken by falling off Bert's lorry before it gets to the warehouse. Use your head, Mr Lamont. How many houses have broken furniture littered about—the type of house with the sort of contents to merit a sale by you, I mean? One of these days, those two porters of yours are going to break up a really valuable piece for sale as secondhand timber—if they haven't already done so."

Lamont rubbed his chin. "There could be something in what you say."

"There *is* something in what I say, believe me. My men assure me of it. They're better at sniffing out that sort of thing than you."

The door opened quietly, and Green came in whistling softly through his front teeth. Masters recognised the signs. Something had gone Green's way. Not a word passed between them. Green sat down and lit a cigarette.

"Can we discuss another of your would-be buys, Mr Lamont?" asked Masters.

"I really don't think I have time for any more of this. I have got some work to do."

"So have I, and mine is far more important than yours."

"What makes you think so?"

"Wouldn't you say it was far more important for me to save you from spending the rest of your life in jail than for you to sit there writing euphoric descriptions of properties for sale?"

"What?" Lamont now seemed thoroughly alarmed. "You can't think I had anything to do with Hardy's murder."

"I can, Mr Lamont, because somebody meant me to."

"Somebody meant you to?"

"Yes, Mr Lamont. In a subtle way, you've had suspicion thrust upon you."

"Rubbish."

"Let me give you just one little bit of evidence to

prove it. The poison that killed Hardy was put into the salad oil in his gimmel flask."

"I guessed that. You virtually told me so."

"What you didn't guess, Mr Lamont, was that the killer had used two gimmel flasks. He primed one with poison, and then substituted it for the one in Hardy's house. Had he left it at that, it is doubtful whether anybody would have realised two flasks had been used, because Mrs Hardy never washed the thing, and it is doubtful whether the thought would have occurred to the police that it wasn't Hardy's original flask. And so they wouldn't have asked the only person who possibly could identify it, to do so. I am referring to Mrs Hardy's home help. But the murderer stole the flask that contained the poison, and did not restore the original one.

"That would have been the logical thing to do, wouldn't you say, Mr Lamont? It would have baffled the police as to how Hardy had been given the poison. But with the gimmel flask missing, it was easy for the police to say how the poison had been delivered. It also meant that the police were going to enquire into the whole business of gimmel flasks. And what happens? We discover that one of Mr Hardy's partners has recently bought a load of glassware among which is a gimmel flask. Of course this partner says that when he came to collect the lot, the flask was missing. But then he would say that, wouldn't he, if he intended using the flask for some nefarious purpose? Do I need to go on, Mr Lamont?"

"No," said Lamont faintly.

"So," said Masters, "can we now get back to another of your abortive efforts to buy through the good offices of Bert Spooner? I'm referring to a medicine chest, *circa* 1840, lot 131 in the March sale. You were prepared to go to twenty pounds for it. Why?"

"What do you mean why? I wanted it to sell again."

"Who to?"

"I hadn't got a buyer. I wanted to get it first, and then I'd have offered it."

"Through Mrs Horbium perhaps, or Mr Benson?"

"I'd thought of asking their advice as to whom to contact—either dealer or collector."

"How did you know it was resaleable?"

"Why shouldn't I know?"

"Mr Lamont, I'm trying to help you out of a hole."

"How? What's a medicine chest I didn't buy got to do with Hardy's death?"

"The chest, nothing. Why you wanted it, everything."

"I wanted to make a bit of money."

"We are well aware that you have been living up to your income, Mr Lamont, and that you're hoping to make a bit on antiques. We know why you went for the gimmel flask—to sell at a profit. Now why go for the chest? How did you know you could afford to bid twenty pounds and then get appreciably more at resale?"

"Because Williams got one at Coleford and resold it for ninety."

"Thank you. Why didn't you ask Williams where he had sold his chest? You might have been able to sell in the same place. And if the purchaser had told you what he would be prepared to give you might have been able to bid a bit higher to make sure of getting it."

Lamont didn't reply.

Green said: "My guess is that you wanted the maximum profit so you told Bert only to go to twenty. Only after you'd got the chest would you ask Williams where he got rid of his, because if you'd mentioned it before, you might have drawn Williams' attention to it and probably brought him into the bidding against you."

Lamont nodded. "If Williams had got rid of one, why not another?"

"Surely, if you said you wanted it, he'd have laid off?"

"Not him. He'd say the client was entitled to as much as we could get for him, and making arrangements to cut out bids was illegal."

"I see. By the way, does Williams collect anything in particular, or does he just dabble?"

"He collects books. Old, technical books. I've not known him go in for furniture much at all."

"Thank you, Mr Lamont. Eventually you decided to be very helpful, which was just as well, because when I came in here I could have arrested you for murder, and I could have made the charge stick."

"Because I tried to buy a gimmel flask?"

"And because of your attempt to buy a medicine chest which contained a supply of the poison used to kill Hardy."

Lamont looked astounded. "Poison? What poison? I haven't any idea what you're talking about. And why just because I tried to buy that chest? You can get poison anywhere. Any garden shed, any chemist, anywhere."

"Not this particular poison," said Masters quietly. "It could not have been obtained anywhere in this country except out of that chest."

Lamont sat astounded. Then he gasped: "But I didn't buy the box. Richard Benson did. I've never been near it to take anything from it."

"We know that, Mr Lamont. But you knew the chest was in the sale, and presumably you examined it before you decided to bid for it. I think you examined it in your warehouse, away from prying eyes. Nobody to see you. Prosecuting counsel could make quite a song and dance about the opportunity that offered you to take some of the poison."

"No," shouted Lamont. "No. I couldn't have taken any at that time."

"Why not?"

"Because the box was locked. There wasn't a key. I didn't see inside until it got to the Corn Exchange. That was when I saw all the things were in it and I decided to bid. Ask Bert. He'll tell you I didn't ask him to bid until lunchtime on the day of the sale."

"Who had the key?" asked Masters.

"I don't know. I thought Bert or Bandy would have it. They always do take keys out of wardrobes and chests of drawers and things, so they don't get lost. The things are locked for travelling and the keys are put back when the pieces are put in the Corn Exchange. But Bert and Bandy said they didn't have the key."

"The box was locked when they collected it from wherever they did collect it?"

"That's what they said."

"Now there's a funny thing. There's still no key to that chest, but it is open, not shut."

"I know. I told you I saw inside at the Exchange. There was still no key there, so I thought I'd been mistaken and the lid had got jammed in the warehouse."

Masters got to his feet. "Never mind, Mr Lamont. Now, if you'd care to come with us. . . ."

"Where to?"

"The police station. No, don't worry. We're not arresting you. We're going to take a statement from you. A very long, full statement. You'll be there until after lunchtime."

"But my work?"

"Your liberty, Mr Lamont."

Lamont gave a resigned shrug. Masters said: "Would you mind driving us there in your car? Then you'll have it with you for coming back in."

"May I just tell. . . ."

"No, Mr Lamont. Let's just keep this a secret between us, shall we? We don't want people to get the wrong idea and to think you're under arrest."

"No! No, I suppose not."

Lamont was shown into the interview room. Masters and Green conferred outside the door.

"Do you really want his statement, George?"

"Most definitely. But I dragged him here with us because I didn't want him talking."

"Who to?"

"Williams. From the way you came whistling into that office I take it you did find a medicine chest in one of the Coleford auctions?"

"That's right. I checked it out. Williams bought it for sixteen pounds. He made a nice profit on it if he offloaded for ninety. Seventy-four quid, just like that."

"He didn't make any profit on it. He made a loss of sixteen pounds."

"What?"

"That's the chest Benson's got."

Green stared, open mouthed.

"That's right," said Masters, "only one chest with croton oil in it. Two would be a bit much, wouldn't it?"

"I don't get it. There'd have to be two if the oil wasn't taken from Benson's bottle."

"No, Greeny. Williams bought the first chest. Took out some of the croton oil, said he'd sold the chest at a fancy price, but in fact, he put it into a house, the contents of which were to be sold at the next auction."

"Why, for heaven's sake?"

"Don't you recognise Williams' style? He tells Lamont that he got ninety pounds for a medicine chest. The next thing Lamont knows is that there's a medicine chest for sale. What's Lamont going to do?"

"Try to buy it on the sly."

"Exactly."

"But all that rubbish about the key?"

"Williams had to make sure that things weren't nicked from the box by Bert or Bandy. So he locked it. He had to open it once it arrived at the Exchange, to make sure Lamont would see it was full and worth bidding for. But he couldn't leave the key in the lock, because it was highly probable that Lamont would have asked Bert and Bandy for it, and he would have been told there wasn't one. So he had to risk that Lamont would accept a jammed lid, which he did."

"Exactly the same sort of ploy he played on Hardy over the development scheme. Subtle, Benson called him."

"Right. And he did the same thing with Lamont

over the gimmel flask. He made sure by hint and in-
nuendo that Lamont couldn't lift the flask but had to
bid for it in public. Then Williams pinched the
bottle. Lamont's story that it was stolen would sound
very phoney to police investigating a murder in
which—as Williams made sure—a gimmel flask was to
play so great a part."

"Too bloody true it sounded phoney."

"Then, I asked Lamont what Williams collected, if
anything. He said old books of a technical nature.
When you search his house, look for an old medical
book or one on pharmacognosy which mentions croton oil, won't you?"

"You're not coming?"

"No, I'll have to leave it to Frimley to be in nominal charge—for the sake of local pride."

"Anything else?"

"Williams could come and go at Hardy's place
without appearing suspicious. He'd know Hardy used
a gimmel flask. So I think it's all tied up."

"I wonder if I can find the key to that chest?" murmured Green.

"No," replied Masters. "That and the flask will be
beyond our finding now. Williams is no fool."

"I don't know. You've managed to nobble him
without even meeting him."

"Still. . . ." Masters shook his head.

"Motive?" asked Green.

"Does it matter? But I'd say if you were the middle
partner of three in a prosperous business, it would be
decidedly to your financial advantage to kill off the
senior man and have the junior one go to jail for life
for doing so."

"I like it," said Green.

"Right," said Masters. "Find Frimley and Hoame and the three of you bring Williams in. I'll get Reed to take Lamont's statement. Meanwhile I've three phone calls to make."

"Three?"

"One to Telford. One to Wanda. And one to your good lady to tell her the weekend is still on, starting tomorrow as previously arranged."

Green nodded his approval.